FINAL SHIPS

IN THE NEIGHBORHOOD

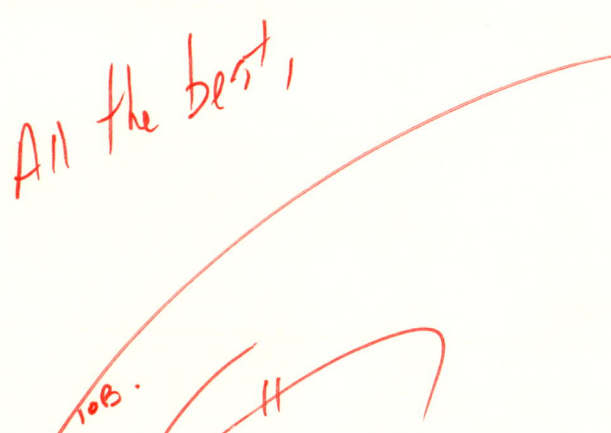

Giant Tales 3-Minute Stories:
Giant Tales Beyond the Mystic Doors (Book 1)
Giant Tales From the Misty Swamp (Book 2)
Giant Tales: World of Pirates (Book 3)
Giant Tales: Dangerous Days (Book 4)
Giant Tales: Wrapped In Fur (Book 5)

Giant Tales Apocalypse 10-Minute Stories:
Lava Storm In the Neighborhood (Book 1)
Final Ships In the Neighborhood (Book 2)
Darkness In the Neighborhood (Book 3)

CRYSTAL SWORD CHRONICLES:
GRYFFON MASTER: Curse of the Lich King (Book 1)

GIANT TALES APOCALYPSE
10-MINUTE STORIES

FINAL
SHIPS
IN THE
NEIGHBORHOOD

Introduction by
**PROFESSOR
K.R. LIMN**

Professor Limn Books
Charlotte, North Carolina

GIANT TALES 10-MINUTE STORIES series
FINAL SHIPS IN THE NEIGHBORHOOD (Book 2)
Anthology Copyright © 2012 by H.M. SCHULDT
All rights reserved.
No part of this anthology may be copied,
stored in a retrieval system,
or reproduced in any manner whatsoever
without permission
except in the case of brief quotations
for articles and reviews.
Professor Limn books may be purchased
for educational, business, or sales promotional use.
Please do not participate in piracy of copyrighted materials
in violation of the authors' rights.
Purchase only authorized editions.

For information, please write to: H. M. Schuldt
www.writers750.com

Cover Art © 2013 by Northlake Art Studio
Interior Art Design © 2014 Northlake Art Studio
Each author holds the copyright to their own story.

First published in 2014 by Professor Limn Books
ISBN 978-0-9885784-8-7

~ PERMISSION ~
Each author from
FINAL SHIPS IN THE NEIGHBORHOOD (Book 2)
owns their individual story and
has given official written permission
to place their story/stories in this anthology for publication.

First Edition, November 2014

THE SECOND TRUMPET

*The second angel
sounded his trumpet,
and something like a huge mountain, all ablaze,
was thrown into the sea.
A third of the sea turned into blood,
a third of the living creatures in the sea died,
and a third of the ships were destroyed.*
Revelation 8:8

Foreword

What do you do when the world around you just isn't right? When mysterious things start to happen that you just can't explain or you see things that just should not be there?

Final Ships In the Neighborhood is a collection of such stories written by many authors that you have come to know well, if you have followed the Giant Tales collection. If this is your first time with us, then we welcome you to join the adventure.

Each *Final Ships In the Neighborhood* author takes you on a unique journey into an unknown world or on a nail biting adventure. As you cherish each experience, you will be touched by each author's individual writing style. However, you will find some common ground. Before the stories were put to paper, the author were given three specific guide posts, referred to as highlights, and one theme to plot their course. The three highlights they were to include are an appointment, a mysterious ship, and a rock or asteroid. The guiding star, also known as the theme, is ambition. The stipulation was to include these things in a story and do so in about 2,000-3,000 words.

Seems like an impossible task? This group of authors would beg to differ. They accepted the challenge in their own unique way and created this collection of stories just waiting for you to enjoy.

LYNETTE WHITE

Contents

FINAL SHIPS
IN THE NEIGHBORHOOD

1. *End Game* by Nina Soden 1
2. *The Tsunami Effect* by Stephanie Baskerville 12
3. *Pyrat Rum* by Timothy Paul 21
4. *A New Day* by Lynette White 33
5. *From Behind the Sun* by Randy Dutton 43
6. *The Appointment* by Joyce Shaughnessy 56
7. *Acceptable Losses* by Randall Lemon 65
8. *The Shooting Star* by Gail Harkins 75
9. *Dragon Ship* by Andy McKell 86
10. *The Mud Race* by H.M. Schuldt 98
11. *The Rise and Fall of King Dabbolt*
    by Laura Stafford 112
12. *The Last Dawn II* by Christian Warren Freed .. 122
13. *The Mystery of the Sinking Ships* by Shae Hamrick 130
14. *Restoration of Order* by Amos Parker 141
15. *Ark* by Andrea Luquesi Scott 155
16. *To Anacreon In Heaven* by JD Mitchell 163
17. *Gravity Up* by JZ Murdock 175
18. *Krima* by Robert Tozer 185

AFTERWORD

Nina Soden
Stephanie Baskerville
Timothy Paul
Lynette White
Randy Dutton
Joyce Shaughnessy
Randall Lemon
Gail Harkins
Andy McKell
H.M. Schuldt
Laura Stafford
Christian Warren Freed
Shae Hamrick
Amos Parker
Andrea Luquesi Scott
JD Mitchell
JZ Murdock
Robert Tozer

INTRODUCTION

In *Final Ships In the Neighborhood*, authors were asked to write a short story set in the future during apocalyptic times. They were challenged to include an appointment, a mysterious ship, and a rock or asteroid. An optional backstory was given where the main character is forced to cancel an appointment for some reason. As an example, two possible reasons were given as to why the character missed the appointment. It could be that a bridge went out or something was blocking the way but, as in all the Giant Tales books, the author has the freedom to decide how they want to build their own plot.

You will find a slight variation in settings. In this collection of short stories, authors were originally presented with a situation where about half of the ships on Earth have been destroyed. Some of the authors chose to set the story on dry ground, while other authors chose to set the story out at sea, and a few authors chose to set the story in outer space. This slight variation keeps the stories fresh and interesting. As in all the Giant Tales books, the authors have the creative freedom to develop a story however they want to. In this book, the authors decide if the main character had something to do with the destruction, nothing to do with the destruction, or if the character can help stop another devastating destruction.

I am very pleased to present another wonderful collection of 10-Minute Stories in the Giant Tales Apocalypse series. These stories are fictional and highly entertaining.

PROFESSOR K.R. LIMN

1

END GAME

by
Nina Soden

There was a moment, fifteen seconds, maybe twenty, right as I was waking up when everything seemed perfect. I could hear the waves playing from the sound machine on my nightstand, and a cool morning breeze was coming in through my bedroom window as my husband's hand gently rubbed my arm trying to wake me up. I had a choice; pretend to be still sleeping and maybe he would bring me breakfast in bed, or rollover and maybe his warm touch would lead to more.

I decided to rollover.

Then reality hit me. My muscles ached as if a truck had hit me. I couldn't lift my arms, my legs, or even my head. My throat was dry and my eyes were too heavy to open. "Mmmmm." I couldn't seem to get my mouth to work right. Words didn't seem possible. "Mmmmm."

"I think she's waking up," I heard a woman say. Her voice was muffled as if she was far away or behind closed doors, but I knew she wasn't because I could feel her hand touching my arm. Her soft, delicate skin startled me. It was no match for my husband's strong rough touch. I tried to pull away but I couldn't move.

"Billy, I said she's waking up."

Billy? Do I know that name? I couldn't place the name or the voice of the young woman talking to him.

"It's time to wake up," she whispered as she continued to rub my arm. "You need to wake up now."

"She can't hear you, Jenny. You're wasting your time."

"She will wake up!" Jenny snapped as she placed a cold wet rag across my forehead. "You need to wake up now." She was getting agitated, maybe even desperate. I could hear it in her voice. She wanted me to wake up…no…she needed me to wake up.

"Nnn…nooo." I wanted the rag off of my forehead, but I couldn't lift my hand to do anything about it.

"Billy, she's waking up."

"She isn't waking up. Look at her. Her eyes aren't even opening. It's just like the last time."

The last time? What did he mean the last time?

"Stop that!" The young woman barked. All of a sudden the cold rag was gone. I heard it hit something, maybe Billy, and then it fell to the floor.

"Don't throw things at me, Jenny! You're acting like a child!" As he got up to stomp away, I could feel the whole room moving, rocking as if we were on a boat.

A boat? Why would I be on a boat? I hate boats. I can't be on a boat. I tried to recall the last thing I could remember, but it wasn't easy with the pounding in my head and the growing nausea I could feel coming on. Just the thought of being on a boat caused instant nausea. I never was able to handle boats, planes, or even long car rides without feeling sick. *I was in bed, wasn't I? No, no that isn't right, I never made it home last night. I had to change the... My car. I was in my car...I had just cancelled our lunch date, and I was...Oh no, Eric... did he get my message? Is he looking for me?*

"Think about it Billy, what are we going to do if she dies?"

What are we going to do if she dies? Her words echoed in my head a thousand times. *What are we going to do if she dies? I wasn't going to let that happen.*

"It's simple, Billy. If she dies, we die! You know he isn't going to let us live if she dies!"

"Nnnoooo... I'm... I'm fine." My throat stung as I tried to speak and what came out didn't sound like my voice at all. "I'm fine. Just... just help me up." With my eyes still closed I tried to reach out and pull myself up, but I still couldn't move. I realized it wasn't because my arms and legs were heavy, but because they were tied together. The ropes dug into my wrists and ankles getting tighter every time I tried to move.

"Oh my god! Billy, help me!" He grabbed me under my armpits and pulled me up, so I was sitting against the wall. "It's time to open your eyes now, Clare."

Clare... that's my name. The idea that she knew my name was comforting, but the fact that I still couldn't place her voice was not.

"Clare, open your eyes!"

"Move out of the way," Billy demanded. I could hear them shuffling about, and then unexpectedly my head was thrown to the side, my jaw crashed into the wall hard, and my cheek stung from the friction as his hand smacked me.

"Billy!"

"Shut up, Jenny. I'm done playing nice. My wife and son are dead because of them. If you want to be her friend that's fine, but I want off this boat. I want my life back, what little I have left..." I could hear the pain in his voice as he tried to swallow back tears. "Like you said the only way that is going to happen is if we get her to him today! So if you can't handle this, you can leave."

"Yeah, where am I going to go, Billy? We're in the middle of nowhere on a boat that ran out of gas four days ago."

Four days ago? How long have I been out? Why hasn't anyone…

"Why don't you just take a little break, Jenny? Go down in the cabin and wait for me."

"You can't—"

"NOW, Jenny."

I could hear her tentative footsteps on the hardwood floor as she slowly walked away, and I could feel what was about to happen a second before he struck me again. It didn't hurt as bad as the second time. Maybe my face was still numb from the first blow. "Open your eyes, or I will hit you again!"

I nodded. I didn't want him to hit me again. I wasn't sure I could take it. "I… I'm trying." It took a couple of minutes but I got my eyes to open. Everything seemed so bright. Looking back, I don't think it really was, but having been out for two days, maybe longer, the sun beating down on me was a strong contrast to the darkness behind my eyelids. I could taste the blood, already filling my mouth and tried to spit it out, but it just ran down my chin instead. "Where…where am I? What do you want from me?"

He laughed. He laughed long and hard as if I had told him a joke. "Are you serious?" Standing up he looked around gesturing to nothing and everything, "ARE YOU SERIOUS?!" He picked up the chair he had been sitting in and smashed it on the floor. A couple of the legs flew at me barely missing my head. Then he threw what was left over the side of the boat. "All of this…everything…it wouldn't have happened if it wasn't for you."

"What happened?" My hands started to tremble and the rope bit into my skin. Tears filled my eyes, not because I was afraid of what must have happened, but because looking in his eyes I was afraid of what he might do to me if I couldn't fix it. "Please, I don't know what you're talking about. What did I do? If you just tell me, I'll—"

"Tsk, tsk, tsk…You disappoint me, Clare." He crouched down next to me pulling up on the rope, connecting my wrists to my ankles, and yanked me away from the wall. I cried out in pain but he didn't stop. "I promise you we will make contact today…" he leaned in close and I could feel his breath on my cheek as he whispered in my ear. "…and when we do, you'll be all his and no one will be able to help you." He dropped the rope and I fell back against the wall as he walked away and down into the cabin of the boat.

***

When I woke up again, Jenny was sitting at my side. "Are you okay?"

I swallowed. My throat was still dry, but it wasn't as bad as it had been and I didn't taste blood anymore. "I have a headache and my jaw hurts." In reality, my whole body ached and my head felt like it was going to explode. "I need something to drink, please."

She held a glass of cold water to my lips, and I swallowed it down as quickly as I could before she took it away. "You'll have to forgive Billy. He doesn't mean to be so rough, it's just that…well, we've been through a lot to get you here." There was a commotion downstairs and she quickly looked over her shoulder at the stair. Billy wasn't there.

"But why?" I reached out and was able to grab her hand. "Why do you want me here? What do you need me for?"

"Hmm…" she peered at me through squinted eyes and shook her head. "Billy said you didn't remember, but—"

"I don't. I swear. Please tell me what happened. How long have I been on this boat? If you tell me what's going on, maybe I can help."

"You can help. You're the only one who can help. None of this would have happened if it wasn't for your…your husband."

"My husband? What does Eric have to do with this?"

Jenny stood up and walked to the edge of the boat. Gripping the railing that circled the deck she stared out across the ocean for a while before finally turning around. "Clare, what does your husband do for a living?"

"He's a software engineer. He works with computers…" Eric had worked as a junior software engineer for a small local firm for years until recently being offered a job as the Senior Software Architect at Global Dynamics.

"A software engineer? Is that what he told you?"

"It's the truth. When I met him, he was designing video games at a firm with an old college friend. He only recently left his position there."

Crossing the deck she grabbed a manila folder off of the table. "Do you know why he left?"

"Of course," I answered. "He took a job at Global Dynamics working with a team of engineers and scientists. They're working to improve the safety of global communications."

"NO!" Jenny shouted. "Are you kidding me? Don't you watch the news?" She tossed the folder at me as news clippings, documents, and pictures fell out covering the floor around me.

"What is this?" I could see photographs of my husband and some other men. Bold headlines on the news clippings read,

> *Global Dynamics develops newest atomic bomb*
> *GPS Guided Missiles Released by Global Dynamics Scientists*
> *Global Dynamics Accused of Launching Warheads*
> and
> *World War III?*

She pulled a knife out of the back pocket of her jeans and swiftly cut the rope that had been holding my ankles together. I was able to stand up, but she quickly grabbed the rope and used it like a leash to drag me across the deck of the boat by my wrists. "Where are you taking me?"

"You really can't be this stupid, Clare. You can't tell me you didn't know what your husband was doing!" She pulled me down the stairs to the lower deck just as Billy was opening the door.

"What are you doing?" Billy snapped. "Why is she walking around?"

"I'm showing her the news recording. If she really doesn't know what he has been doing, then it's time to open her eyes!" She yanked me past him and through the door. Shoving me down onto a couch against the far wall, she grabbed a laptop off of the table and pushed play on a recording that was already opened on the screen. News flooded the screen with images of fallen buildings, collapsed bridges, and large freight ships and military vessels ablaze with fire in the middle of nowhere.

I could feel tears starting to fill my eyes. "What? Where? Where is that? When did this happen?" I couldn't blink. I couldn't look away. It was like the world was falling apart all around us, yet we were a thousand miles away.

"You're telling me you didn't know?"

"I didn't know what?"

"Eric Flisher, your husband, he built the missiles that did this." I shook my head. It couldn't be true, but she just continued. "He has launched sixty-three missiles in the last four days, killing hundreds of thousands and destroying more than sixty percent of the military and trade ships globally."

"No, he's a good—" I couldn't believe what she was saying. I just stared at the images on the television each one worse than the one before.

"YES!" Billy screamed from across the room as he slammed the door shut and locked it behind him. He scowled as he slowly closed the gap between us. "To be honest with you, Clare," he spit my name like it tasted disgusting in his mouth. "I don't care if you knew about any of this or not. Getting information out of you would have been great, but really all I want is for this to stop and the only way that is going to happen…the only chance we have at finding him is if we draw him out, and the only thing he wants is you. So, guess what that means…you're the bait and it's time to fish!"

"Me? But, if he did these things you say he did… I don't want—"

"I don't care what you want! We've already made contact and everything has been arranged. His ship should be here soon. When he gets here, you'll go with him." He pulled me off the couch and spun me around. I could feel something

8

cold being pressed against my back as he lifted my shirt. "With this tracker, it shouldn't take long for the few remaining navy ships to find you." He turned me around, so we were face-to-face. "But if you warn him…if you tell him you're being tracked, I won't hesitate to give the order to kill you! Do you understand me?" I nodded hard and fast. "Good girl." Then shoving me toward Jenny he said, "Get her ready! We haven't got much time."

***

They cleaned me up; wiped the dried blood off my face, gave me clean clothes to wear and even a meal to eat. The food wasn't good. If I was going to die, it wasn't what I would have hoped for as a *last meal*, but they didn't give me a choice.

The sun was just setting as we stood on the deck of the boat waiting. It seemed like we waited for hours before I could finally see his ship in the distance. As it got closer, I could see the words *Global Dynamics* clearly printed along the side of the ship. *HONK! HONK!* The ships horn blared into the night air echoing around us.

HONK! HONK! Billy repeated with the considerably smaller horn of the boat I was being held captive on.

I turned to Jenny who, like a statue, stared out at the oncoming ship, one hand on the railing and the other on the gun held at her side and pointed at me. "Please, please you don't have to do this."

"One life to save thousands…" She turned to me. "I'm sorry. I don't have a choice."

The ship stopped fifty yards out. I could see people bustling around on the deck of the ship, but couldn't make out their faces. I knew this was my only chance, and I took it.

There was a large rock on the table, being used as a paperweight, about eight feet behind us. If I could get my hands on the rock I could get the gun from Jenny, but I had to do it quickly before Billy got back.

I slowly backed away from the edge of the boat. "You do have a choice. You know I didn't have anything to do with this, you could save me if you wanted to." I was almost at the table, and she was following me just as I had known she would.

"I don't know that." She kept her gun aimed at my chest. "Even if I did, I couldn't save you without sacrificing thousands of others."

"Please." I turned toward the table and slouched down as if crying. "I'm begging you, please don't do this." She didn't see me grab the rock and she wasn't expecting it as I turned fast hitting her right in the temple. Slowly at first and then more quickly, blood started to flow from the gash on the right side of her face and she went down with a heavy lifeless thump. I grabbed the knife out of her back pocket and quickly cut the remaining ropes from my wrists. Then with her gun in my hand, I made my way to the railing and stepped over.

"Don't do this, Clare." I heard Billy pull back the slide of his gun and release it. I knew without looking back that he had a loaded chamber, and it was pointed directly at me. "I will fire, Clare."

HONK! HONK! The ship's horn bellowed again.

"NOW!" It was Eric's voice cutting through the distance from the large ships speaker system.

I turned back smirking and whispered *goodbye* to Billy. His eyes widened as he realized I wasn't so innocent after all.

I leapt from the side of the boat. Just as I hit the water, the missile hit the side of the boat. I saw it explode, sending shards of wood all around me.

The small rescue raft was at my side in minutes pulling me out of the cold water.

***

Standing on the deck of the Global Dynamics' ship, I watched as the last of the fires died out and the scattered boat scraps floated by. Eric stood behind me and wrapped his arms around my waist. "Hi."

"Hi yourself." I turned in his arms, and we were face-to-face only inches apart. "You know, the plan was that I would be held in the warehouse off the dock. Not on some rickety little boat!"

"It was a fifty-foot yacht, Clare, not a row boat. Besides…" he turned away. "There was a complication with the warehouse."

"What kind of complication?" I stepped back.

"Nothing I couldn't handle." His eyes met mine. He knew what I was thinking. Even though I loved him, I wouldn't hesitate to kill him if he messed up. He knew I would do anything to make sure this mission was successful. "You really are one ruthless woman, aren't you?"

I closed the gap between us and wrapped my arms around him. "I don't know. I like to think of myself as ambitious." With a simple kiss on his lips, I took his hand in mine. I led him into the belly of the ship. "Come. We have work to do."

An Afterword to this story is on page 197.

2

THE TSUNAMI EFFECT

by
Stephanie Baskerville

If I hadn't been so engrossed in *her*, I would most likely have been able to stop the devastation. That sounds so harsh to admit...harsh, because it shows how selfish I was. And oh, how the earth has paid for my selfishness! Several areas of the world are now underwater, whole civilizations lost. All of Central and South America—gone. Australia, half of Africa, half of Europe—annihilated. India, Indonesia and Japan—completely destroyed. And all the states and provinces along the coasts of North America—wiped out. All blanketed by the rushing walls of water from the tsunamis that formed from the asteroids that collided with Earth.

I stare out from the balcony of my eighteenth-floor Fort Worth, Texas condominium, contemplating the vastness of the two-week old unnatural ocean as it literally stretches as far as my eyes can see. San Antonio, Laredo, Houston, Odessa, Midland, Dallas, and several other cities now lie underneath the new ocean. Most of Texas is underwater now, in fact, but at least in Fort Worth, all the buildings around me are still standing. However, most of those buildings are now buried in water up to the third floor. My own building, for instance.

From my vantage point, I can see two sunken cruise ships that I can only assume had been docked somewhere, maybe in California, or maybe Florida, before they got pushed inland… just two of several of the cruise line casualties. Their large white corpses have, however, assisted us. Some of us who survived were able to salvage life boats from the ships as they drifted past us, so at least we can travel around the city now. We also salvaged scuba gear, once used for tourists aboard ships who wanted to learn the sport. Now that equipment comes in handy when we need to do a canned food run. After all, our supermarkets are underwater, too. Just like everything else.

The sunken ships remind me that the cruise lines weren't the only ship-building industry hit by my gross oversight. At last count, three-quarters of *all* the ships had been destroyed. Of the remaining ships, less than half of them are still functional. The United Nations commandeered those remaining working ships to be retrofitted as rescue ships, and then sent them to search for survivors. So far, the reports haven't been good. Just more guilt to add to my heavily burdened shoulders.

I could have stopped this from happening! I could have easily detected the asteroids, if I'd only been paying attention. But *she* dominated my existence. *She* took every moment of any free time that I had…time that should have been spent watching the skies. *She* was truly a magical creature. There isn't a detail that I can't bring to mind just by closing my eyes and remembering *her*. The feel of *her* under my hands was like touching silk. Every curve of *hers* was laid bare for my thirsty eyes and I never got tired of her beauty, no matter how many times I looked at *her*.

* * *

Dr. Jonathan Enders...that's me. A former astronaut, but a freak accident left me grounded. Kind of anti-climactic for me, what with my double PhD in Astrophysics and Geology, yet I can't bring myself to go up there again. They say that there are several people who would give their eyeteeth to be working on a Space Station. Well, I'm no longer one of them. Not after my near death experience in space. Debris had hit my thruster pack and damaged my portable life support system while I was outside the shuttle. I was stranded with no way to get back to it, and my oxygen was fading fast. The accident should never have happened. After all, they're supposed to design these suits to withstand debris! If it hadn't been for my partner...

Even though I refused to go back up there, I still couldn't get the longing to explore out of my blood. So Mission Control offered me the job I hold now, or rather, I *held* before this terrible turn of events. I was responsible for monitoring the skies, watching for anomalies that might affect us here on earth or affect the astronauts in space. I *should* have been doing my job, two weeks ago.

I grind my teeth in frustration, beating my hands impotently against the balcony railing. I can't escape the thoughts; the constant nagging is with me every minute of the day. The haunting *what ifs* that keeps rolling around in my head. A groan of anguish rips from my weary soul.

I should never have canceled that meeting! I cry inwardly. *Why? Why was I so stupid? What would have happened if I hadn't canceled? Would the devastation be as extensive if I'd reacted differently? If I'd only been able to warn everyone ahead of time, would the death toll be as high as it is now?*

It's something that I cannot bear to contemplate. Yet I'm tortured nonetheless with the images of the destruction that was wreaked on the world in such a short period of time. All because of me. And my relationship with *her.*

My treacherous thoughts turn toward *her.* She was always so alluring to me. She beckons to me in my mind even now, through all the guilt. But I can't bring myself to go see *her.* For me, that guilt is just too raw. I don't even know if she survived, to be honest. I shy away from the thought that she might not have survived…although I can't go to see her because of my guilt, the thought of losing *her* is even more unbearable.

You are obsessed. A part of me tells myself. The inner voice sounds cynical. *You didn't even care that much after you realized that Sharon wasn't coming home!*

Contrary to the inner voice, I wince away from that thought before the tears can start to fall again. Sharon, my beautiful wife…lost forever under the waters along with the rest of civilization. Another stab of intense pain knifes through my heart and I bite back a scream of anguish.

My oversight killed my wife *and I'm worried about* her? *What kind of monster am I?*

Sharon and I, sure, we had our differences, especially after the accident. I wasn't the same person and she tried her best to help me. Tried much harder than I deserved I'll admit.

She took me to all those psychologists, insisting that one of them could help me. I think to myself. *She was so dutiful. And in my misery, I pushed her away. Always pushing her away. Just like I pushed her away two weeks ago.*

I want to wince away from the memory but I can't. I shake

my head, disgusted and ashamed of myself for the last encounter I had with Sharon. If I hadn't been so obtuse, so bent in my own fantasies about *her*, Sharon would never have left the condominium. She'd still be alive right this very minute, home safe with me, if I'd just listened to Sharon and forgotten about *her*.

I had spent all of my time with that thing! I'd been packing my things to go to *her* again. The duffle bag had been out as usual. Sharon had come up behind me, without my hearing, with the same complaint as she always had: spending my time with *her*.

"Why aren't you ever here when I need you?" she'd asked.

"I've already told you. Working on *her* is the only relief I get!" I had snarled back at Sharon. This time, there were no tears. Not like before. This time she had just sighed heavily and shook her head.

"I don't understand who you are anymore. I've tried. I really have. But I just don't get you. Look, go work on your project, then. I'm going shopping," she'd said. That cut deep but I refused to let her see that it had.

"Fine," I had replied.

"I love you, Jon." Her voice had been soft. I grunted a grudging reply.

"Yeah, sure. Love you too."

Why had I said that to her with so little feeling? Why couldn't I let Sharon know how much she actually meant to me? The questions are tormenting my mind. But I know the answer. I know it all too well.

Because after my accident, I was always too focused on her *to be able to pay attention to my wife. My project had come first. Not Sharon.* I try to dislodge the cynical thoughts with a violent shake of my head.

"No!" I moan. My hands clutch convulsively on the

balcony railing, the sides biting into my palms. But my conscience has has just spoken the truth and I can't deny that fact. "Sharon... oh, Sharon!"

I sink to the ground, a tear falling from my eye, another following it. The iron railing of the balcony suddenly looks like prison bars.

I should be in prison. I think to myself. *Think of all the people I've killed!*

The water below seems to beckon to me. It would be so easy just to throw myself over the balcony into its blue-green embrace.

But I can't. I deserve to suffer. I don't deserve any mercy. And if there's a way I can stop this from happening again, I must do it. I think I owe that much to Sharon.

I move slightly, using the railing to stand once again. I stagger inside, heart wrenching with the sudden need to understand what had happened. What had I missed? I had cancelled the meeting, yes, but *why* had I done so? I must not have thought that the threat was real.

I head into my office. The pictures taped to the wall were taken a few days before the asteroids hit Earth. Those asteroids look huge to me now. But I see my notes, formulas and observations scribbled in red, over each of the pictures. I'm reminded of why I thought I could blow off the meeting to go spend time with *her*. The trajectory of the asteroids ensured that we were in the clear.

Why had they shifted? Why had the asteroids, which should have cleared Earth's atmosphere, hit us at all?

My phone rings, but I ignore it, staring at the pictures on my wall until the answering machine picks up.

"You have reached the voicemail of Jonathan and Sharon Enders. We are unavailable to take your call right now. Please leave a message with your name, number, and the time that you called. We will return your call as soon as we are able. Thank you."

I need to change my answering machine message. Hearing it gives me another stab of agony and guilt that Sharon's not coming home.

"Sharon? Sharon, it's Mom. I'm returning your call from yesterday. What's happening? What's going on? Why aren't you at home with Jonathan?" The voice of my mother-in-law on the phone and what she's saying shocks me into listening. I stare at the machine. "When you get this message, give me a call, will you? Sharon, I love you honey. Whatever's going on, I'm sure you and Jonathan can work it out, and your father and I are here to support you. If you could tell me where you are, well, never mind. We'll talk about that when you call back."

Sharon's alive? I feel my eyes opening wide. *She's alive and she hasn't come home?*

Do I really blame Sharon? My cynical conscience is back and I wince.

No. A tear slides down my cheek. *Sharon probably thinks I'm with* her.

I'm seized with a restlessness that will not go away.

This is a sign from above. Nancy must have thought that she was calling Sharon's cell phone. Now that I know Sharon's alive, I can't leave her wherever she is. I need to go find Sharon. That's it. She has to know that she comes first in my life.

Abandoning the photographs and calculations plastered on the wall of my office, I head resolutely toward the bedroom to pick up my duffle bag. It's still packed from that fateful day two weeks ago. I look into it and see tools, a change of clothing, some granola bars, other non-perishable foods, and some bottles of water. Everything I need to go work on *her* will now be used to go find my wife. It's a perfect parallel, I think. My mind is racing. *Where was the government taking survivors?* I'm sure I'd heard that somewhere.

They're airlifting people that they find! The answer comes to me in a flash. *They're taking them further inland!*

Galvanized into action, I throw the strap of the duffle bag over my shoulder, grab my keys and my cell phone, and stride resolutely towards the door.

I'm dialing her phone even as I begin the long walk down the stairs of my building. I get her answering machine.

"Sharon, it's Jonathan. I know you're alive, and I don't blame you for not coming home. But I'm coming to find you. I'm so sorry! I'm so sorry about everything. I'm sorry I let something like a mere sailboat get in the way of the love you and I once shared. You were right. You were always right. I need to put this accident behind me and move on. And I'm going to let the hurts from the accident heal. I might need your help, but if you can forgive me, I'll maybe begin to forgive just a little part of myself. I'm coming to find you. Please, call me back and tell me where you are. I love you so much. More than anything. I'm so sorry that I was blind to that before." *Why am I babbling?* So I say a final 'I love you,' and hang up. I'm almost at the bottom of the stairs and can hear the water slapping against the concrete.

A small flicker of something that I recognize as hope blossoms in the pit of my stomach. With it comes something else…the conviction that I will not rest until Sharon has been found. And my project, my thirty-two foot sailboat that I've been working on, is going to help me find Sharon.

I resolutely close the door to our condominium. It is time. Time to go see if the *Midnight Mischief* is still operational. Time to go find my wife. Time to fix what damage I've done. Time to deal with things like a man.

It is time to start living again.

An Afterword to this story is on page 198.

3

PYRAT RUM

by
Timothy Paul

Chris Nash looked down at the White House as the Navy chopper flew southeast from Langley. Their flight plan followed the western coast of Chesapeake Bay down to Norfolk. In the seat ahead of him, the pilot's body language was rigid and tense—alert. Chris glanced back for a last look at the White House.

"Weren't you supposed to receive your award today?" the young operative sitting beside him asked.

She'd been assigned by the Director of National Intelligence, John Salinas, but that was all Chris knew about her. "Yeah," he nodded. "That's the kind of meeting that gets postponed once and after that, an endless cycle or rescheduling." *My one chance for a handshake with a sitting President*, Chris thought. He needed to get over his disappointment and focus.

"Sorry," she replied.

Had he said that out loud? He shot her a quick smile. "No sweat. I think of it this way. It took an invasion to keep me out of the Oval Office."

"Invasion?"

Regardless of her inflection, the surprise in her eyes was genuine. The directorate thought enough of her talents to assign an operation far above her pay grade but hadn't elevated her clearance to let her know her life may soon be on the line.

"Don't you think that's a little over the top?" she asked. "We're passing through a meteor shower."

Chris's eyelids shut as he stifled a grimace. "What's your clearance level?"

"Top secret."

They're always so proud their first time out, he thought. "You've read the morning briefs and a half dozen news reports?"

"I've reviewed numerous briefs and read news reports from seven different countries. At this moment I may well be the world's leading expert on the phenomenon," she retorted.

"What have you read about the maritime losses?"

"Several military and civilian vessels have been struck. There are two reports of damages severe enough to sink a ship. Both were tankers. One German, one Saudi."

"How many of those 'Top Secret' briefs mentioned the fact that every rock to fall through the atmosphere strikes a waterborne vessel?"

"That hasn't been detailed in any…"

Chris watched the self-assured expression melt from her face. "Simple meteor showers don't have targeting devices," he said. "Nor does a softball sized rock fall from space and bore a hole into a destroyer all the way down through the hull."

"Ookaaay," she acquiesced. "How many ships *have* we lost?"

"In the past twenty-four hours, nearly half our surface fleet have sent distress calls and issued orders to abandon ship. London and Ottawa have appealed to us for assistance with similar numbers."

"Other countries?"

"Not everyone is sharing information so openly, but intel suggests every naval force on the planet is getting hit."

Forty minutes later the two NSA operatives sat in a private war room briefing from Admiral Gusset. Behind the Admiral a large monitor displayed a global map showing real-time positions of ships. Lots of ships. Arrows, vectors and flags appeared by each vessel as they would during combat operations.

"Our submarine force is tied up with rescue efforts," the Admiral detailed. "But it takes time to surface and time to clear the decks and submerge. Experience has already taught us we have almost a seven minute window from the time the boat breaks water until it must start the dive sequence again."

"Why are we here, Admiral?"

Gusset shot her a somber look. "I have no idea how *you* were chosen. But Colonel Nash has a background with extra-terrestrial investigations, and this is a two-person assignment."

"It's Agent Nash, Admiral. I retired from the Marines three years ago, as you well know. What do you need from us, Admiral?" Chris asked.

"We need to know how these space rocks can sink ships. The first step is getting a closer look."

"A closer look?" the girl asked, apparently unintimidated by the Admiral's patronizing.

"We're running point." Chris glared at the Admiral. "You want to put us on a boat, wait for it to get hit, recover a sample – assuming it hasn't shot clean through the bottom hull – then somehow get off the boat and bring the thing back here." To this point in time, his investigations of unexplained events had always followed a reported incident. He was not excited about being used for bait in an active assault.

"That sums it up, Colonel. We've assigned a skeleton crew to man a decommissioned frigate. You'll be shadowed by a submarine whose only mission is to pull you out – with your sample."

"In other words, if we don't signal the sub, 'Item in hand,' they're not going to risk surfacing."

Gusset nodded grimly. "She's fueling now for a short run. Once you're five miles out, if you haven't been hit yet, you'll be sailing up and down parallel to our coast."

"Will we have a shielded sample box?" asked the young woman.

Chris looked at his inquisitive partner. "Shielded?"

"Something is falling from beyond our atmosphere and we don't know anything about it. If these meteors emit substantial levels of radiation . . ."

"The sub will have proper storage. For the retrieval phase, you'll be issued radiation strips."

"At least we'll know what we're facing," Chris glowered.

With nothing more to add, the two were dismissed. Chris looked at his young associate. Her face had paled significantly, and there was a noticeable absence of swagger as she strode down the corridor. "First field op?"

She nodded, took several breaths, then answered, "I didn't join the agency because it's a safe place to work."

He was pleased to see she had a healthy dose of fear. "I know it's a bit late to ask your name, but the day's gone faster than most. Even for me."

"Agent Morris, Sir."

"Ms. Morris, we've just been ordered into hell together. My name's Chris, not Sir."

She nodded. "Okay, Sir." Then she corrected herself adding, "Chris." Only when he raised his eyebrows did she catch his full intent. "Staci. Staci Morris."

"Well Staci Morris, if we both come back from this, I've got a bottle of Pyrat dark rum waiting for the right occasion. I invite you to share a toast to success."

Tension in the corners of her mouth eased and turned slightly upward. "I accept."

Two hours later they stood on the aft deck of the USS Ford, anxiously watching the shoreline recede in the distance. Soon the frigate turned north maintaining a five-mile distance from the coast. Chris maintained direct contact with the Virginia-class sub that mirrored their course.

They sailed until the ship was even with Massachusetts without incident. An anxious captain decided they were playing things too safe by hugging the coast. He contacted the Pentagon and received approval to turn east and set a course toward Her Majesty's Naval Base Devonport.

"There's a tactical intelligence to these things," the captain explained to Chris. "Either they're not watching anything this close to shore or they've looked at our route and determined we're not worthy of attention."

Chris noted his use of the third person plural as well as the strategic jargon. "And you think we'll make a more obvious target if we navigate toward foreign soil?"

"I'm not sure they would have a way to determine England is a separately governed territory, but it certainly looks more like we have a maritime intent crossing the ocean than we do skirting a single continent."

Confirmation of the captain's hypothesis followed before U.S. coastal waters were fifteen miles behind. The first collision hit with ear-shattering abruptness and no warning. "I thought you had tracking devices looking for these things!" Chris hollered as he ducked for cover.

"We're watching the sky with everything from radar to infra-red. So far, none of these have shown up on any of our monitors. Didn't the Admiral tell you?"

"Must have slipped his mind!" Chris shot out of the wheelhouse and slid down a ladder to the quarterdeck. One level below, Agent Morris ran toward the impact point near the Ford's bow.

A second strike rocked the boat backward. The third gave Chris his first visual impression as it struck the main deck directly below him. Its force of impact was formidable. The after-effects were subtle but no less spectacular. Moments after impact, wisps of steam rose from the rock, or...was the deck of the boat evaporating?! Geometrically shaped with regular angles, the device exposed the precision of designed engineering, not natural phenomenon. A fourth strike somewhere on the port side rocked the ship followed by a fifth hit to starboard. He stared through the vapors of the nearest, memorizing every detail of the device until a hole formed and it fell through to the deck below.

The initial strike had come at evenly spaced intervals and struck the extremities of the ship as if mapping parameters for a targeting system. Now, a monsoon of destruction rained down on the frigate. Chris spotted Staci huddled under a winch housing and prayed it would hold up. Speakers blared the Captain's order to abandon ship. Chris frowned with disapproval as the frantic sailors rushed toward lifeboats hanging just outside the barrage. From his current vantage point, he witnessed two men die trying to reach safety.

Hugging the forecastle, Chris suppressed vivid memories of firefights in Iraq. Meteors, rocks, and weapons were strewn across every level of the ship like baseballs in a batting cage.

Barely a minute passed before vapors rose in random patterns and holes formed all around him, dropping buckets of devastation down to the next level. By the time he could focus his phone's camera on the event, the frigate's main deck looked like the surface of the moon. He moved across to Staci who was peering down one of the holes and rubbing her hand around its edges.

"The steel looks like it's been melted," she said. "But the metal's cool."

As they looked on, the event repeated itself on the level below. "Only a few of them are making the holes," Chris observed. "Then the rest drop through. Like a programmed sequence."

"I've been watching that batch," Staci added. "It looks like each piece carries a single charge of…whatever melts the steel." As she spoke, a new hole formed on the level below them and the devices pelted the next deck. Sounds like marbles dropping on a tin roof echoed around them as other holes formed. "Look there," she shouted. "One of them hung up on the next level."

"We don't know if it's dormant. It may be waiting to blow its charge further down."

"Yes we do. I've had my eye on that one. See the left edge. Most of the sides are convex. That one's concave. None of them have that shape when they first strike. I think this one's shed its payload."

"That's a long shot of a guess."

"We have to retrieve one, right?"

She was right, but none of the holes nearby were wide enough for him to fit through. "I'll make my way down. You stay here to guide me to the right hole."

"That could take time," she said. "We don't know how much we have."

Before Chris could object, the girl slid her petite frame through a hole and dropped to the level below.

"Check your radiation strip."

"I have. It's clear."

He peered down the shaft as she cautiously lifted the device from the floor.

"It's heavier than it looks," she shouted. "About twenty pounds I'd say."

"Can you work your way to a ladder without falling to another level?"

"It's a bit of a maze, but I see one I can reach. Shouldn't take long to get back to your level."

"Meet me on the port side. I'm going to have a look at the aft deck to see if I can find another sample or two. Soon as you're back I'll call for extraction."

It didn't seem possible but the rear of the boat was even more cratered than the fore section, but luck was with him. As he rounded the back of the superstructure, a hexagonal object lay directly in front of him. Hard and heavy, the substance reminded him of a small fragment he'd found at a site in Northern Minnesota ten years earlier. No lab had yet identified the composition or even determined if it was alloy or element.

FINAL SHIPS IN THE NEIGHBORHOOD

With his sample in hand, Chris contacted the submarine. "People from Ford's crew are in boats south of the ship. I have a sample. Moving over to rendezvous as soon as I collect my partner."

He met Agent Morris as she climbed back to the main deck with a metallic object, slightly smaller than his own. They made their way starboard and began lowering a lifeboat when time ran out. A new shower rained down on the rescue ship. Submariners worked with rapid precision to load the surviving crew but three more deck hands were crushed before the rest were inside. Already holes were forming atop the sub. They could not submerge and there was no backup plan for escape.

Chris jumped at a series of sudden explosions above him. The latest assault had taken a serious toll, but now the masses of devices were exploding in midair. *Are they unstable?* he wondered as he looked at the alien object in his hand. Flashes like those from a gun muzzle preceded each explosion. Something was shooting them out of the sky, and it came from the opposite side of the frigate, out of sight of the submarine.

With eyes fixed on the fireworks display above, Chris ran to see the source and nearly fell through a hole. No other vessels were authorized in this zone, yet there it was. It bore no markings. Structural features were clearly military, but its class and configuration, even the shape of the boat, was unlike anything else afloat. It looked like an American Naval cruiser that had been sliced in half lengthwise. Half a dozen machine guns on its foredeck spit tracers into the sky. Each round found a mark, obliterating one of the falling devices. Every strike made a distant pop and that's when he noticed it—the guns made no sound at all.

29

Agent Morris caught up to him in time to see a brilliant flash to the rear as a missile emerged from a tube in the aft deck. Shielding his eyes, Chris turned his head away from the sun-like brilliance until it was a fading speck high above. A moment after the rocket's flames disappeared, another blinding flame filled the sky. The mystery ship's guns stopped firing and nothing more fell toward them.

Moving at speeds that seemed to defy physical laws, the strange craft pulled alongside the frigate and stopped abruptly. Chris's secure phone came to life. "Captain?" he answered.

"Yes, Colonel Nash. I am the captain, but not the one you expect."

"Then I assume you're on the vessel in front of me."

"I am."

"What is this boat? And what is your armament? And how do you know my name? For that matter, how do you have this number?"

"I'm sure you can deduce answers to those last two questions, Colonel. I'm not at liberty to tell you anything more."

"At liberty?! I've got a level…"

"Save your rant and indignation. I understand and sympathize, but no one else must see this vessel. We have two minutes to take Agent Morris aboard and be on our way."

"What?" Chris looked at the girl suspiciously. Her wide eyes and blank expression told him she heard the same conversation through her earpiece. Apparently she knew nothing more than he did. A ramp shot across the narrow expanse bridging the two boats. "How do you know about her?"

"She was requested for this project based her specific aptitudes and a lack of any living family. There was a reason she was assigned to accompany you."

"So Director Salinas knows about this project?"

"Director Salinas knows less than you. Send her across the bridge, now, with the devices you recovered. Otherwise, this recruiting session is over and we will be forced to sink the Ford with both of you aboard."

He placed a hand gently on Staci's shoulder, shook his head and said, "We don't know anything about them."

"You will be her point of contact, Colonel."

Staring down at the ramp Staci said to Chris, "It's okay. Besides, you owe me a toast. This is a chance learn about things beyond our world."

"You may not like the things he wants to show you."

She looked up at him with the sort of expression a circus daredevil might wear just before leaping through a ring of flames. "I'm curious," she said. "And maybe a little ambitions."

Before Chris could respond, she walked across the bridge, stepped onto the mystery ship and disappeared into the hold. The ladder withdrew and the ship pulled away.

"Your superiors and the crew of the Ford must think she has been killed in this assault," the captain said.

"What's this about?"

"They want our waterways."

"If I'm her point of contact, how do I reach her? Captain?" he called. No response. He shouted at the ship as it pulled straight away to the north, then began a turn toward— nothing. As if sliding behind a vast, invisible curtain, the misshapen vessel just disappeared.

He'd spent fifteen years investigating UFO reports. It was enough to convince him something or someone possessed technologies far beyond our own. But nothing before this ever suggested hostile intent. Despite misgivings about the mystery ship, he felt certain Staci Morris would contact him soon. And it wouldn't be for a glass of Pyrat rum.

An Afterword to this story is on page 199.

4

A NEW DAY

by
Lynette White

The citizens of Kinonville and Kingston shared an old National Guard Base with five thousand other survivors. Angie Williams, former mayor of Kinonville, sat on the governing board with two other mayors, the governor, and a federal senator. The law enforcement was turned over to Chief Dan Davis, Sheriff Jake Winters, Sheriff Sam Jackson, and Chief Andy Pearson. They trained the new police force and maintained peace in the camp.

The civil leaders worked tirelessly to stabilize the chaos. This freed up the army officers to concentrate on searching for survivors, scavenging for supplies and food, and reestablishing communication with the rest of the world.

Angie pushed herself far beyond her limits and it was taking a toll on her. Her endless optimism had been strangled by the demands of the day-to-day survival. Today was one of those days when she was on the edge. She stood with her arms crossed beside Chief Dan Davis, watching twenty people sitting in a field less than one hundred yards in front of them. They were a group of fanatics that Lieutenant Colonel Jack Mcquire rescued ten days ago and brought here to Camp 11MW.

From the moment they climbed out of the trucks, they started preaching that the quakes, tsunamis, and volcanoes as well as the destruction of 60% of the world's population was just the beginning. The newest disaster was going to be asteroids, and they would cleanse the earth right down to the last blade of grass.

Angie was out of patience with them. "Why are those nut cases sitting in the middle of a field?"

Dan shrugged his shoulders and sighed. "They are claiming the first asteroid will strike right here in a few hours."

She threw up her hands in frustration. "Good, I hope it better not miss *them*," she growled.

"Now Angie, you don't mean that," he gently reprimanded her.

Her arm shot up, pointing at the group in front of her. "Those people are nuts, Dan! I am having a hard enough time without nut cases like them stirring up people who are already terrified," she declared and dropped her hand.

Dan agreed these fanatics were just making a bad situation worse. "Angie, I know you are frustrated, but wishing people dead is not like you," he remarked.

Angie lowered her head and sighed. He was right. She never used to be like this. Her mind drifted to the first few hours after Kinonville was destroyed by the earthquake. She spent two days going from house to house rescuing any survivors. What happened to that Angie Williams?

Looking up she apologized. "You're right, Dan, I am sorry. I just need some time to clear my head before General Condin arrives. I will be in my apartment if you need me."

"Will do, Boss."

She made her way back to the tiny three-room apartment she shared with her ex-husband Alan Brighton. Since fate brought them back together, they were slowly working through their stormy past. It was not easy for them to openly admit they still loved each other, but their hearts finally won over their heads.

Alan ran one of the salvage teams and was gone for days at a time. It was a mixed blessing to have him gone so much. He returned a few hours ago, but must have been busy unloading the trucks. Angie was honestly glad to find the apartment empty. She went straight to their bed, plopped down, and was sound asleep within minutes. The slamming of the door woke her up with a start. Before she fully comprehended what was happening, Alan was standing beside the bed.

"Angie, we have got a problem!" he announced.

She closed her eyes and turned away. "I have a long list of problems, Alan. Just give me another twenty minutes and I will see what I can do."

He sat down on the bed and pulled her onto her back. "Angie, I mean a real problem. Like an alien problem. We spotted the ship two days ago, but it followed us. It's less than fifty miles from here. One of our trucks broke down and when we went back to get it we spotted the ship."

She forced herself up onto her elbows. "What are you talking about, Alan? You sound like those freaking nuts out in the field waiting for an asteroid."

She dropped back down on the bed and covered her eyes with her arm, "On second thought if I am lucky, your aliens will abduct those fanatics. That would take care of twenty of my problems."

Alan was exasperated. "Angie, baby, I am serious."

He stood up and tried to pull her off the bed, "Just come with me and see for yourself."

Glancing at the clock on the wall she pulled away from him, "I can't go anywhere, Alan. General Condin will be here in less than a half hour. Do you have any idea how angry he will be with me if I blow him off to go chase some mysterious space ship? Besides, they are flying in. So if there is something out there they will see it."

"By then it'll be too late," Alan pointed out. "They are coming in from the north and the ship is coming from the south. They will not see it any sooner then this entire camp will!"

"Then go tell Lieutenant Colonel Mcquire," she suggested.

"I tried. He is nowhere to be found. I should have told him as soon as I got back. We didn't know it was following us until we went back out to get that truck," he persisted.

She finally heard the honest fear in his voice and sat up. "You are dead serious about this."

"Yes, Angie. I am dead serious and you are the only one who will have access to the lieutenant colonel and the general today. You have to come see this so you can tell them what is going on."

She gave up and slid off the bed. "Alright, alright, let's go see this spaceship of yours. But you better pray they are hostile. If they don't kill me, the general will for being late to this meeting," she added as an afterthought.

"I am praying no one dies today, baby, and especially you," Alan said, pulling her out the door.

They jumped into his jeep and sped out of camp. As they rushed toward the unknown, he explained how they came across the ship hovering over a rock outcropping. Alan sent the trucks on, but he stayed behind with two other men to observe the mysterious craft. It moved no more than a half-mile during the twenty minutes they watched it. Finally, it dropped down behind the rocks. A bright light reflected off the rocks for a couple of minutes before it rose up and shot off to the south. At that point the men rejoined the caravan.

A flash, from the sun reflecting off a metal object, caught their attention. Alan sped toward a group of rocks. They tucked the jeep away and grabbed two pair of binoculars. Alan and Angie climbed up to the top of the rock formation and flattened their bodies against the rocks, raising the binoculars to their eyes.

Sure enough, hovering about 200 feet above the ground was a small craft. It was round with a large windshield. It was slowly moving forward, but didn't make a sound. The light reflecting off the glass made it impossible to see who was manning the craft. The sun's reflection off another metal object drew their attention to the ground. Moving below the craft was a dozen little robots, about a yard in height. They resembled little snowmen with fully functional hands and tank-like treads instead of feet. Three of the robots were pulling wagons while the others slowly began to separate into groups of three. One of the *wagon pulling robots* followed each group as they dispersed.

When the groups reached their predetermined positions, the three robots gathered around the wagon. Each one grabbed a stake and a mallet from the wagon. Splitting up again, they started to pound the stakes into the ground. When each stake was in place, the little bot touched the side and the top of the stake opened up. A small light rose up and started flashing. Some of the stakes flashed red, some blue, and some green.

"What are they doing?" Angie whispered.

"How am I suppose to know?" Alan countered. "But do you believe me now?"

Angie lowered her binoculars. "Yes, you are right. We need to warn General Condin."

They crawled off the rocks and scrambled back to the jeep. Angie was still shaking when she jumped out of the jeep and ran inside the makeshift command center/city hall. Sitting with the general was the lieutenant colonel, five other officers, the civil leaders, and Dan Davis. The conversation stopped the moment she rushed in.

"Well Mayor Williams, how nice of you to finally join us. The meeting started over an hour ago. That is a bit beyond being fashionably late." General Condin greeted her in a gruff tone.

"I apologize for being so late, General Condin. I have been with Alan investigating a potential threat to this camp."

All eyebrows went up, so Angie pushed on. "We have a problem heading our direction. There is some sort of floating craft to our south with little robots. Those little bots are planting stakes." Her mouth snapped shut when the general leaned back into his chair and laughed.

All eyes moved from Angie to him. "Oh the geo bots," he sputtered. "About time those boys got up here."

Now Angie was furious. "The...the...*geo bots*? What is a geo bot?"

The general pointed to her vacant seat. "Sit down, Mayor Williams."

Angie didn't move. "You mean to tell me you know what is out there?"

Now he nodded toward the chair. "Of course, I know what they are. Take your seat, please."

It was not a request this time, so Angie moved toward her chair and sat down. General Condin waited for her to get settled before explaining.

"What you saw is a prototype, developed by some of the brightest minds in physics, geosciences, robotics, and space engineering from around the world. Their original purpose was to study global warming.

"The intention was to use the geo bots to enter into unsafe terrain and plant the research spikes. That information is fed to the scientists hovering safely up in the craft.

"The blue spikes feed information about water levels. The red is *seismic activity*. The green is read *air quality*. There are also others that read air pressure, wind velocity, etc."

He paused to catch his breath. "Six prototypes were finished and were being tested when everything went bad. Only two of those were not damaged. Two more were salvaged and are being repaired. Once they are fully operational again, they are off to Europe and Africa. Instead of global warming, we are using them now to look for safe places to rebuild humanity.

"Their information will help us know where to start rebuilding permanent cities again. The scientists can cover about fifty miles a day so it is slow going. They are focused on the inner areas of the states as those areas had the least amount of destruction."

Everyone was astounded. Angie was still irritated. "And why didn't you tell us about this?"

Lieutenant Colonel Jack Mcquire tapped the papers in front of him. "For your information, Angie, we were just getting to that. It is right here on the ole agenda for today. We knew they would reach this area soon, so we were going to give you a head's up. We didn't want people to get alarmed when they saw it. It seems…"

Angie raised her hand to cut him off. "Whoa! Whoa! You mean to tell me you knew about this, too, and never bothered to tell me?"

"Now wait a minute, Angie, I found out about it three days ago myself and I have been a little busy," Jack defended himself. "Besides, I knew it was going to be discussed today. What I didn't know was that Alan's team would come across it first.

"Thank God he didn't raise an alarm about it. Those fanatics out there waiting for the asteroid to hit them have caused enough disruption without the fear of an alien attack too."

Angie was not going to back down that easily. "And that is just supposed to make this alright? What if someone else saw that thing besides Alan? Jack, I have told you time and time again to alert me about stuff like this!"

"Angie, I am sorry," Jack apologized.

"Now, Mayor Williams, this is not something to get all upset about. You are overreacting here just a bit," the general jumped in.

She was not about to be insulted. "Not to get upset about? Do you have any idea how tense these people are right now?" she retorted.

General Condin slowly leaned forward, unmoved by her temper tantrum. "Mayor Williams, you are trying to run *one* camp of 5,000 people. From what I have heard today you are doing a superb job, and I commend you for that." His hand moved to cover his heart. "But, I have *nine* more camps just like this one I am in charge of."

His hand moved to span the room. "You are dealing with 5,000 terrified and tense people. I am dealing with ten times that in what use to be eight different states."

"I have been to the Pacific Ocean which is now almost to the Sierra Nevada Range. I have also been to the Atlantic coast. It has reached to the Appalachian Mountains. The Gulf of Mexico flows over most of what use to be Florida.

"North and South America are now separate continents. From what few reports we have received, it seems thousands of miles of coastline around the globe has vanished. Entire mountain ranges have split apart. Rivers all over the world have simply disappeared or flow miles off course. Not to mention, entire islands have vanished into the seas.

"I have overseen the disposal of millions of bodies and witnessed destruction you can't begin to imagine. So no, this is not something to be upset over."

Angie suddenly felt childish and ashamed at her outburst. She hung her head and tried to force away the images he just planted in her head. "I am so sorry," she whispered.

The general leaned back in his chair. "All is forgiven, Mayor."

She slowly looked up. "How do you ever maintain any sense of hope?"

General Condin knitted his fingers together and tapped his tented index fingers thoughtfully against his chin. "I have hope because I have learned some surprising things about the human race the past few months, Mayor Williams. We are an amazingly resilient species."

He pointed his fingers toward Angie. "You know how many babies I have held in the last couple of months?" he asked but did not wait for her to answer.

"Hundreds. And as I looked into their tiny little faces, I realized something. They will know nothing of the world as we knew it. Only as they know it."

His hands dropped to the table but did not separate. "As I looked at those babies I came to understand that as long as we have hope, we will be just fine. As long we are willing to change and adapt, we will survive. It is not the end of humanity, my good lady, but the beginning of a new chapter in the story of the human determination to survive. We may be in the middle of a dark night right now, but the next dawn is coming. All we have to do is believe and hold on until those first rays peak over the mountain."

Angie smiled and more than one person in the room wiped away a tear. She could feel her perspective shifting back toward the Angie she used to know. The Angie who took on any challenge knowing she would somehow overcome it.

"You are right, General Condin. I have almost forgotten how to have hope. Thank you."

The general actually smiled. "Good, glad we got that cleared up. Now let's get this wrapped up and have that news conference before anyone else sees that ship."

Everyone nodded and the general cleared his throat. "Alright, Mayor Williams, let's get you up to speed."

An Afterword to this story is on page 200.

5

FROM BEHIND THE SUN

by
Randy Dutton

Nine blinding flashes, each five seconds apart, flooded SpaceGuard's telescope.

Despite the optical dampening controls, Celeste instinctively stepped back from behind the press barricade. Her widened eyes rapidly blinked from the nuclear intensity directed at an asteroid officially designated as *2016DA22*. Unofficially, astronomers called it *Whiro* after the Maori lord of darkness and embodiment of evil. The nickname fit—it was on a collision course with Earth.

The pert Global Heartbeat News reporter gazed at the operation center's activity. She slowly turned from the action and looked past the other eight pool reporters—everyone was science-educated except her.

Celeste pursed her lips, reflecting on her new venue. The long, curved command center was rotating to maintain a modicum of artificial gravity. It provided a changing background.

Stark. Not quite the luxurious casino setting I'd planned for. It's so industrial! Not a red carpet in sight.

Only yesterday she had ascended the 100,000-kilometer long carbon tether from the space elevator station, located over equatorial Indonesia. This was her first trip to space and she had spent half of the two-day transit too excited to write anything but poetry. The view from the elevator pod captured her breath as the blue planet fell away and the sparkling stars became more brilliant. That was before her boss's email changed her assignment and forced Celeste to bury herself in scientific research too alien for her to fully grasp.

Why me? She silently pouted. *Just because we had a press slot?*

Her eyes paused at a blacked-out display. Moments before, it had shown telemetry. Her peripheral vision kept track of the whiz kid assigned to her. A courtesy SpaceGuard provided help to ensure her science reporting was accurate.

"Effect?!" Director Smith called out. The tall woman stared at the computer image of the 3-kilometer long cylindrically-shaped crystalline rock. Like a dog chasing an intruder, this earth-trailing asteroid was coming closer.

"One missile detonated prematurely," Weapons reported. "Nine direct hits."

"Ma'am, Whiro has slowed to 4km/sec. Deflection was minimal," Ops called out. "Sensors show Earth's gravity is accelerating it again."

"Was it enough?" the Director asked.

"No, Ma'am! Earth impact now calculated in 37 minutes. We gained 11 minutes. New incident angle at 30 degrees…impact zone, coastal Somalia."

"Sensors, any major break up?"

"Primarily rock clusters, nothing larger than 50 meters in diameter. Whiro's mostly intact."

"Reload for another barrage! We moved Whiro's impact from the central Indian Ocean to land. We have to shove it more!"

"Director, if we fire all remaining 10 missiles, we won't have any for large pieces that break off," Ops cautioned.

"I'm aware of the risks but if we don't deflect this beast, pieces won't matter. Tell the UN to send us more nukes ASAP!"

Weapons typed a few commands. "Canister's ready. Target acquired. Ten rounds on your mark."

The Director looked at Weapons. "Fire!"

Like ducks in a row, a computer screen displayed ten animated missiles heading from the space elevator's Trump Station to Whiro's solar side leading edge.

"Why's the fifth screen black?" Celeste quietly asked Calderon, her NASA escort.

The 25-year-old redhead flipped his iPad to a screen and his fingers tapped several keys. He turned to her. "Seems an energy beam shot off Whiro and hit a sensor. Probably the reflected energy of a nuke."

"The asteroid fired back? How's that possible?"

"Whiro's made of large, flat diamonds that reflect and refract energy and shoots it out in very tight beams—"

"Like a lens?"

"Like a laser. Probably why the approaching missile blew up."

"You know, I've reconsidered. This is far more exciting than covering Trump Station's tenth anniversary!"

Calderon's eyes shifted from scanning the monitors, to his attractive 26-year-old charge. He smiled at how her Gucci pants suit showed off her figure. "Interviewing the space casino's glitterati was your original assignment?"

"Yipper."

"Boorriinngg. But it explains the outfit. Nice pumps," he added referring to her footwear.

"Thanks. Elegant and sweats were all I packed." The corners of her mouth curved up and her cheeks rose. "I don't usually cover science, but our original science geek…" Her lips momentarily pursed. "Sorry, I mean our guy got sick."

"Well, be glad you're not on Earth. It's going to be havoc down there for quite awhile." He pointed to the main monitor. "Okay, here's the moment of truth."

The room was deathly quiet as the viewer displayed eight sequential flashes. The Director tensely yelled, "OPS! REPORT!"

"Two missiles vaporized. Eight hits." Ops paused as new data arrived. "Telemetry shows that Whiro deflected out of a direct Earth impact." The room started cheering. "New projections are that it'll go into earth orbit. Current velocity about 5km/second."

The Director's shoulders relaxed and she exhaled noticeably. "Debris?"

"Whiro's mostly intact, but a field of rubble is approaching Earth. Meteors will commence entering the upper atmosphere in 10 minutes."

Celeste leaned toward Calderon. "Why isn't the Director happier about the asteroid not hitting Earth?"

"Because Whiro's orbit will be unstable. Like the Sword of Damocles, it might fall down on their heads, though thankfully, not at the speed it would have without the nukes. That could have been an extinction event."

"Oooohh, a philosopher."

"Personally..." He looked into her pretty, upturned face, then his eyes drifted to her tablet. "Sorry, I shouldn't be offering unapproved sound bites."

"Okay, off the record." She lowered the electronics.

His attention shifted to the Director, then back to Celeste's green eyes behind her tortoise shell glasses. "I think we have a great opportunity to study a phenomenon. This thing was in Lagrange 3—"

"What's that?"

"A stability point in Earth's orbital path on the far side of the sun, hidden away like a Trojan horse. Theoretically, Whiro should have stayed there as it follows the circular orbit of Earth."

"Why'd it move?"

He shrugged. "We think it's a combination of external and internal forces propelling it forward. The energy beams it emits have prevented us from getting close, but sensors show a powerful trail of ionic particles. I've speculated it has an inner diamond tube that creates a natural ionic engine."

"How would that work?"

"If Whiro's hollow, perhaps some of the sun's energy is penetrating the crystals and ionizing material in the tube. The effect's a beam of energy."

"A flashlight?"

He chuckled. "Well, not so much visible light. It creates a focused ionic beam out the back end that ejects at nearly the speed of light."

"A light engine. Fascinating! So, equal and opposite reaction stuff. Why doesn't Whiro move faster then?"

"Because there's resistance in space—solar wind and gravity and inertia. Ionic engines provide low thrust but high efficiency. We've never encountered a diamond-encrusted planetary object before. We'll know more soon."

"A woman couldn't invent a more enticing asteroid...looks kind of like a cracked glass vase. What made it?"

"I think it's a volcanic tube from some long-gone carbonaceous planet that broke apart. It's hard to say because most of the probes we've sent up have been destroyed by one of its millions of solar energy beams concentrated by the diamonds."

"How big are the diamonds?" Her ear-to-ear grin and sparkling eyes showed her primary interest.

Calderon chuckled. "I doubt your science guy would have asked that. Some have three-meter diameters. Think you can wear that?"

She lightly touched his forearm. "I could try," she jested.

Calderon's cheeks flushed. "The diamond market will crash if this is harvested. There's more in this thing than all the diamonds on earth."

She dipped her head and looked through her eyelashes. "Still sparkles!"

The bemused guide pointed back to the control room.

"Director," Sensors reported. "Whiro's currently captured in Earth's orbit just inside geostationary orbit and mostly over the equator."

"Make sure our shields block the beams. Not much we can do to protect Earth's surface," the Director responded.

"Roger," returned Sensors. "African and European stations now reporting major damage from atmospheric meteor explosions and meteorite strikes. All 45 infrasound stations now reporting sonic explosions."

Calderon noticed Celeste's eyes narrow. He softly said, "The Nuclear Test Ban Treaty Organization listens for low-frequency nuclear explosions. It also works for measuring large meteor explosions."

Her red head bobbed while she wrote some notes.

Communications added, "Ma'am. Electromagnetic interference is building from the debris penetrating the ionosphere. I'm routing communications through the space elevator tether."

"Sensors. Any chance a piece will hit the tether?" the Director voice expressed concern.

"None yet, ma'am. Space tugs are on standby."

"Good. Let's hope we don't have to deploy the spare. It's hard enough when communications are normal—"

"Director," Ops interrupted, "sensors picking up thousands of flashes per second in the satellite belts. Looks like space debris is being vaporized."

Celeste whispered, "That's a good thing, isn't it?"

Calderon's index finger rose to pause her comment while he listened to Ops reporting. After a moment, his finger dropped. "Now then. Yes, zapping space debris is good, however, the high energy levels mean we're going to lose a lot of satellites, maybe most of them over time. Remember, this thing is weaving and shedding more crap than it's eliminating."

"Oh," she bit her lower lip. "I hadn't considered that."

"The debris will make space travel more hazardous. And, it gets much worse."

Her brow lifted. "How so?"

"The beam intensity means aircraft and even ships are at risk. Think of a million lasers cutting across the sky and hitting the land and water. Fires will break out and the infrastructure's vulnerable."

"Didn't they ground all aircraft?"

"Most of the commercial airlines but some will fly during the quiet times and at latitudes that experts *think* are safe. Many more will be damaged on the ground."

"Any way to mitigate the effect?" Her eyes were full of sympathy.

"Beam intensity will vary. Atmospheric light refraction, dust and cloud cover will help a lot. Reflective covers and shelters are recommended. When Whiro passes into Earth's shadow, it'll go dark, as it's doing right now. And when it's directly overhead at noon, most rays will reflect out to space."

"So how do we stop this thing?"

He shrugged. "Experts are working on that now."

"Aren't you one of them?"

"Yes."

"Shouldn't you be with them instead of me?"

"I stay informed. Besides, you're good company." He winked.

She gently placed her hand on his arm. "Calderon, since Whiro's going dark for a few hours, let me treat you to dinner in the casino restaurant."

"That's the most expensive—"

She squeezed a little tighter and batted her eyes. "I'm a reporter, remember?" She held up the GHN credit card. "Company pays!"

* * *

While sitting in the casino's rotating coffee shop the next morning, Calderon cradled his coffee mug while looking into

Celeste's concerned eyes. "Personally, I think this asteroid's going to motivate more people to move off Earth. An hour ago, Whiro completed its first full orbit. Everyone's paying attention."

She looked at her tablet. "My news feed's down. How bad's the damage?"

"Significant. Beams have damaged half the aircraft on the ground and nearly anything that was flying. A lot of ships were damaged or sank. Communications are sporadic."

She sighed. "And the people?"

He looked down, then into her slightly puffy eyes. "Not everyone could get to nonflammable cover. But, at least the smoke from the forest fires is diffusing some of the energy beam."

Her right hand reached out and covered his left. "What's SpaceGuard going to do?"

"They're still pondering options."

"Which are?"

"They just landed a team on Whiro to survey it and place sensors. They've got several portable nukes in case they find an opportunity. We'll know more in six hours after they lift off."

"Why can't they stay?"

"Command's afraid they'll get hit by a reflective beam when Whiro comes out of earth's shadow. Once we analyze the samples, we'll have a better idea."

"Can't they paint the thing so it doesn't absorb light?"

"They've discussed it, but it would take months to get the right stuff up here and, frankly, a coating probably wouldn't adhere. They've even considered taking a space sail and shrouding it."

"Wouldn't that work?"

"Too translucent. Enough solar energy would pass through to vaporize it from the inside."

"How about blowing it up?"

"They're thinking it's their best option, but that would send extremely large pieces toward Earth. The UN is bickering about the timing and which countries would be devastated by impacts. And honestly, the last nukes weren't very effective."

"Can they shatter the diamonds?"

"All 10 square kilometers of them?" His right hand put the coffee cup down and affectionately covered her hand still resting on his left. "Uh, Celeste, they're diamonds...the hardest materials known."

"Oh, right...not just pretty baubles." She looked down at her coffee and sighed. "Too bad you can't just put more power into its light engine and send it packing."

His prolonged silence surprised her.

He was gazing at the ceiling with open, silently moving lips. A smile was forming and his hand tightened over hers. With a wide grin he leaned over, excited, and kissed her lips. "Celeste, you're a genius! Come with me to the control room!"

Her brow furrowed as his hand pulled hers into the white walled curved room.

"Director, I want you to meet Celeste. She's a GHN reporter—"

"Calderon, I don't have time for interviews."

"Ma'am, she gave me an idea that I want to pass by you."

The Director sat down. "Make it quick. We've got a team on the asteroid surveying it for weaknesses."

"Can we get some nukes inside the tube?"

"Your theory about having a tube running almost the entire length was spot on, but they haven't tried going..." Her brow furrowed. "Why?"

"Project Orion."

"Excuse me?"

"Early 1960s, General Atomics did research on using small atomic explosions for space flight. It didn't progress because of radiation fears. We don't have that problem in space."

"We've been considering using nuclear explosives to blow it up. So?"

"Whiro has an extremely tough diamond shell. The 17 high-yield nukes didn't crack it."

"A lot of the energy reflected off the surface."

"Exactly. If the core is of similar material, which I'm betting it is, it'll withstand a few low-yield nukes inserted into it. Why not use them to propel Whiro out of orbit? Put one, a third of the way in; the second, two thirds in; and the last, all the way in. Time them one hundredth of a second apart: one, two, three. All the energy will expend out the tail. The first will widen the chamber for the next, and so on. If its natural ion engine stays intact, it'll accelerate forward. If we put a fourth high-yield nuke on the leading corner and detonate it after it's out of Earth's gravity field, it'll nudge Whiro permanently out of Earth's path."

The Director stood up and turned toward a computer schematic.

"Not powerful enough to break it up, but enough to kick it forward into high gear. We'd have to do it while it's still dark, before solar ions start flowing."

She smiled for the first time in weeks. "The plan's ambitious, Calderon. You know, that might work." The Director glanced at the clock. "We have four hours before the sun hits it." She turned toward Ops and roared, "Change of plans everyone! I want three 40-kiloton nukes inserted into the guts of that monster ASAP!"

"Ma'am?" Ops' brow furrowed.

"You heard me. We don't want that thing torching another pass around Earth. Let's motivate that demon forward and out of orbit!"

"Yes, ma'am!" Ops replied as she strode to a group of engineers.

Calderon gently took the speechless reporter's hand. "Come with me, Celeste. You've earned a seat in Ops."

"But...I...I'm not sure what I did."

He squeezed her hand. "You inspired me." He turned and their eyes met. "I'm going to call this asteroid propulsion attempt...*Operation Celeste*."

Calderon led her to his workstation and pulled up another chair.

With a quick scan, she quickly noticed he didn't have girlfriend photos. Her eyes lifted to him expectantly. "And if it doesn't work?"

He grinned. "Have a boyfriend? If it screws up, we'll name it after him."

She squeezed his hand and smiled. "Works for me!"

During the nearly four hour lead-up to Operation Celeste, Calderon briefed her on technical issues he knew she'd need for what he referred to as her *Pulitzer story*. He also briefed her on which officials she should interview. He'd make sure they made the time. Occasionally, Calderon left to talk to Ops and the Director, and to get refreshments for his guest.

The new couple filled momentary lulls by talking of family and reassuring each other of their safety. As the countdown neared, they became more subdued.

When the animation showed the asteroid approaching the edge of Earth's shadow, the Director bellowed to a silent room. "Survey team has left Whiro! Countdown has started!"

The projected clock ticked down. *Three. Two. One.* Computer screens showed a flash from the asteroid's body, a bright, prolonged flare shooting out the end of the lurching, tubular rock. As the sun's rays made the crystals glitter, beams escaped, mostly to empty space.

"Trajectory shows Whiro traveling at 11km/second and leaving orbit!" Ops called out. "I think we've done it, folks!" He cleared his throat. "Operation Celeste is a success!"

Everyone in the room, including the other reporters, rose and turned to Celeste, applauding the embarrassed woman.

Celeste slowly stood.

Calderon pulled a small, hand-sized box out of his desk and faced the reporter. "On behalf of SpaceGuard Command, we present you with this token of our appreciation."

Celeste, still overcome with emotion, opened the lid and swooned into his arms. "It's...beautiful!"

"About 539 carats uncut...just a shard to remember us by."

An Afterword to this story is on page 201.

6

THE APPOINTMENT

by
Joyce Shaughnessy

I hurriedly got into the car and checked my makeup. After buckling in, I decided to try my luck on the freeway. Although I lived on the beach in Miami, the quickest way to get to the dock from Allen's house was the freeway.

It was 8:15 a.m., right during rush hour. If I hadn't checked my emails last night before going to sleep, I would have completely missed this meeting. I write a monthly article for a big New York magazine, and I knew how lucky I was to have the job. My hope was to someday publish a book, a romantic mystery, and I had almost finished it.

Mrs. Farber was my editor, and she had written that she was on a cruise ship, which had docked in Miami and wanted to meet me this morning at 8:45. This whole thing was really weird. Who calls a meeting at 8:45? Why not just 8:30 or 9:00? Oh, well. If it hadn't been for my mother, I wouldn't even have this job.

FINAL SHIPS IN THE NEIGHBORHOOD

I lived in my parent's house on the beach. There was no way I could have afforded the place if it had not been passed down from my grandparents to my parents and then to me. I had lived with my mother for twelve years, and then she had passed away. I had helped my mother write the articles for the last ten years of her life, and I was lucky to do it on my own now.

After telling Mrs. Farber that I was a divorced mother of two young children, I think she took pity on me and decided to trust me with the assignment.

Look at all this traffic! I checked my watch and five minutes had passed without so much as a movement. All of a sudden, I heard a horn blaring behind me. I looked up, and there were at least two car spaces between me and the car in front of me! How did that happen? I stepped on the gas and caught up. The guy was still blaring his horn at me. I turned around and mouthed, "Shut up!" He shot me the finger! I couldn't believe it. How rude can you be?

I was pretty sure that "be kind to others" was one of the Ten Commandments. I wasn't sure about it though. It had been a long time since I had seen that movie with Charlton Heston, but "be kind" must have been one of the commandments.

I was so tired of people who were rude. It seemed to happen more when they were driving than anywhere else. We all sat stuck right where we had been before, and that guy hadn't gained more than 5 seconds by blaring his horn at me.

I wondered what Mrs. Farber wanted, or was it Farmer? Was Farber a Jewish name? I wasn't sure. What difference did it make anyway? I'd just stick with, "Hello. It's finally nice to meet you." If her name is Farber and she is Jewish, would she expect me to say "Shalom?" I laughed at myself. Of course she wouldn't! That was just plain silly. Besides, if I said *shalom* to her and her name was Farmer, she'd think I was crazy! I'd stick with my original plan.

It made me think of that man that had lived next door to us—I mean *me*. His name had been Jacob, and I'm pretty sure he was Jewish. He hadn't had a single cross in his house, and that's always a good sign. I had been extra friendly with him just so he'd help me get the house appraised at a lower value, and so he had helped me. It always helps to know who to brown nose. He worked with the city and had contacts. Anyway, he hadn't said *shalom* to me, so I felt my original decision with Mrs. Farker was the right one.

The beach house was important to me because I had inherited it from my dead mother, whom I lived with because she had been so sick before she died.

Some guy in a Toyota was trying to edge in front of me. I honked and yelled, "Jerk!" out my front window. Some people have no manners. He sure didn't know what was on those tablets that Charlton carried.

I started thinking about the mysterious meeting with my editor, Mrs. Farker, again. I hoped she didn't ask me about my sick mother and how she had died. That was a difficult subject for me. Okay. I never did have a sick mother. I had an old boyfriend whose sister had the sick mother who wrote for the New York magazine. His name was Fred, the guy I mean. He wasn't much of a boyfriend, but his sister's sick mother had been a pretty good writer at least. I had met Fred's sister, Lucy, at a writer's meeting. Lucy wasn't any better at writing than Fred was…well, I'd prefer not to think about it. So I decided to make friends with Lucy after she mentioned to the group that her mother worked for the big magazine in New York and was sick. It never hurt to make contacts.

Lucy proved a hard nut to crack. I thought if I befriended her since no one else in the group liked her and she didn't appear to have any friends, she would automatically warm to the thought of my helping her mother write the articles. She wasn't as friendly to me as I was to her. So I made friends with her brother. He was the one who suggested to his mother that I could help her out. I was friendly with him long enough to make sure his mother would let me write with her.

I was pretty sure that being "kind to others" was on the commandment tablet. I had been kind to Fred, Lucy, and their mother, Joan. I probably could have had Joan fired if I had really tried. All I would have had to do was convince Mrs. Farker that I had been writing the articles all on my own. I was following the Heston commandments though. So I just waited for Joan to die before I told Mrs. Farmer that I was a widowed mother of two young children.

Okay. I lied to her about that, too. I don't have any children. And I've never been married, but I know what it feels like because I can imagine what it would be like to live with Fred. It would have been like being trapped in a marriage for all eternity.

So I told a small white lie and appealed to Mrs. Farbler's sensibilities. It worked. She gave me the job, and I've worked pretty hard at writing that monthly article. Even if "no lying" had been one of the commandments, mine had been a harmless lie. It hadn't hurt anyone. It's not as if I had given her the wrong social security number or had committed a felony. At least I don't think two car accidents constitute a felony. And they hadn't been my fault anyway. If Fred had been a better boyfriend, I wouldn't have been angry with him and driven into a light post.

That was when I needed a lawyer. I decided to be his girlfriend, too. His name was David, and just because he had been cute and funny, I decided to let him handle my case for free. He was great in court and he believed my story. I didn't have to do time or anything. I told him that I was a single mother of two young children, and he appealed to the judge for mercy. Of course, she had said she felt compelled to tell me that I should never leave my small children alone in the car. I would never do that! What on earth was she thinking?

It was David who actually lived in the house that his grandparents and parents had left to him. It was a wonderful place. We always sat out on the balcony at night and watched the beautiful ocean. The sound of the waves and the way the salty air smelled were absolutely magical.

We were in a relationship together for a year before David got mad at me and told me he was breaking up. I told him since he was a lawyer, he should know how *marriage by gossip* worked. At least I was pretty sure that was what it was called. We were married as far as everyone in the neighborhood assumed we were. That was how *marriage by gossip* worked, or was it *marriage in common*? Something like that. After all, *marriage by gossip* had prepared me for my future and now I know a few things about the law.

David told me I was out of my mind and he wanted me to be out of his life. I had to find another lawyer. Yes, I had to be his new girlfriend, too, but it was necessary. I was pretty sure David had found a new girlfriend already. Those commandments said it was wrong to leave your wife. After all, I was his wife.

I had my new lawyer, Allen, ask around the neighborhood. I had been absolutely correct. They all assumed we were married, so Allen had made up divorce papers and I had

FINAL SHIPS IN THE NEIGHBORHOOD

David kicked out of his house. Right is right. The divorce court judge took into consideration the fact that I had a dying mother.

That made me think about the meeting again. What time was it now? I looked at my dashboard clock and discovered that it was 8:30 already. I'd never make it on time! I was really upset. *I just can't be late for this meeting.*

That was when I noticed that we weren't just creeping along the freeway. We were stopped and some people were even leaving their cars and running down the breezeway! I turned on the radio to see if there was anything special on the news. I had turned the radio to NPR because I had been forced to pick Allen up at his office last night. I didn't want him to know that I listened to country music. Allen was always finding something to criticize me for and I knew he'd make fun of me. So we had to listen to that NPR crap until we reached his house.

I was seeing Allen about two nights a week. That was going to stop, too. I couldn't stand him any longer. Yes, he was a good lawyer, but that doesn't discount the fact that he's only 5 feet tall. Frankly, I was embarrassed to go anywhere with him. I thought that my tolerance had been amazing, but it had come to an end. I wasn't going to see him any longer.

So NPR was on the radio, and some guy was talking about an asteroid hitting the earth. That's crazy! It sounds like that Orson Welles thing or was it Lawrence Welk? Oh, well, it really didn't matter. I had to find out if it was the truth. The announcer was talking about an asteroid approaching the earth. He said it was huge, about ten miles wide and that the scientists were predicting that it would hit somewhere near the Florida coast, maybe the Florida Keys.

Oh no! Maybe I should run, too. I certainly couldn't drive anywhere. We were stuck on the freeway. It wasn't fair. I was basically a good person. I didn't deserve to die. I could even see the ship where Mrs. Fobbler was waiting for me, a single parent with two children and a dead mother.

I thought about what I had accomplished in my life. I had been writing an article for a big New York magazine after taking over for a dead woman. I had accomplished that all on my own, after being Fred's girlfriend for six months. I deserved something for that, maybe even an Oscar. I had almost finished my book. Well, at least I had written the first chapter. I had tried to obey the Ten Commandments as depicted so well by Charlton Heston. I was normally kind to others and didn't lie except when absolutely necessary.

I decided that the only thing that made sense was for me to just get out and walk to the ship. I could see it anyway. All of those stupid people walking away from the ocean weren't going to get far enough to make any difference. Maybe I'd get lucky and it wouldn't hit me. Maybe I would get *really* lucky and it would hit the ship before I got there. I really didn't want to meet that woman, whatever her name was.

I held my head up high and walked down the breezeway, certain that God would spare me. I knew I was meant for greatness.

Then I heard a loud explosion and the ground started giving way beneath me. The freeway was breaking in half like in an earthquake! I was falling toward the ocean when I managed to grab a portion of a freeway light pole that was almost broken in half. I tried to pull myself up when I saw someone reaching for me. It was a man holding onto the freeway and trying to reach me.

I reached for his hand, and he yelled, "Hold on tight. I'll pull you up."

My whole life flashed before my eyes in those few seconds. I thought about the Ten Commandments and how I had always been a pretty good person, as well as a pretty good writer.

The stranger managed to pull me up to safety, and I put my arms around his neck. I said, "Thank God you helped me. You saved my life."

"That's what I do for a living, ma'am," he said in a southern twang. "I'm a Dade County fireman."

He sounded just like the D.J. on my country station. I thought to myself that I had finally met the love of my life.

Then I looked out over the ocean. There was a huge boulder and it had landed in the water, causing the water to gush toward the causeway like a flood. Unfortunately for Mrs. Farber, it also landed close enough to her ship to cause it to upend, like in the movies when people get stuck on a ship that was sitting upside down. The odds were against Mrs. Farber coming out alive. I wondered vaguely who would get Mrs. Farber's editing job for that big New York magazine.

The fireman said, "If you'll just let me carry you, ma'am, I'll take you to safety. I don't think the asteroid caused much damage to anything but the water and that one ship."

I asked, "What's your name?"

"It's Randy. Randy Hughes. What's your name?"

"Olivia Stone. I'm a writer."

"You're the prettiest woman I've ever rescued."

"Thank you. I guess I'm okay for a widowed mother of two young children and a dead mother." I heard myself telling him that and bit my lip.

63

Randy said, "Well, I'll be. I'm a widowed father of two young children, too. What an amazing coincidence."

I heard myself saying, "It's like we were meant for each other."

He said, "Yeah. I mean, I can always divorce my current wife, who isn't the mother of my two children. I think that our love has been written in stone, like that one carried by Charlton Heston in that movie. Do you know what I'm talking about?"

"Yes. Will your two young children have to live with us?"

"Nah. They really never existed anyway."

"I live in a beach house that I inherited from my dead mother."

"There's something about 'not lying' that's written on those tablets that Charlton Heston carried. I'm glad I told you the truth."

Then my true love carried me to safety.

Everything was perfect, unless he found out my plans for moving to New York. After all, I couldn't let a perfectly good editing job opportunity simply pass me by, especially since I had two children to support.

An Afterword to this story is on page 202.

7

ACCEPTABLE LOSSES

by
Randall Lemon

Captain Harlow Anders now commanded the Voidrunner ship recently renamed *Restitution*. He knew in his heart, he was unworthy of that command. But ever since the Kifari attack on Earth, the Space Force had been pressing a number of unlikely candidates into service.

When the Kifari attacked Earth, they destroyed half the existing ships and knocked out every single shipyard so that making new ships would be impossible for a while. That blow would have been devastating enough on its own. However, spies had informed the Kifari forces of the locations of all the base officers' quarters as well as the enlisted men's housing. The gunners aboard Kifari ships targeted those gatherings of officers and men, with pinpoint accuracy, destroying 75% of active officer personnel and inflicting equal damage on the enlisted.

Young Lt. Anders would have been among the dead except for an act of incompetence that forced him to miss a

10:30 a.m. appointment at the Officers Review Board. Anders knew that the board was considering disciplinary procedures and perhaps dismissal, based on his less than lustrous career in the Space Force. He had intended to be on time—trying to defend his indefensible mistakes—but he had gone off base to have his uniform cleaned and pressed. When he returned to his car that morning, uniform in hand, he noticed he had a flat tire. He opened his trunk and realized that he had forgotten to replace the *doughnut* after his last flat. Feverishly, he called base and asked them to postpone his hearing until he could get a replacement tire.

They told him to forget the tire and take a cab. But try as he might, he couldn't find one and then his cell phone ran out of juice. By the time he finally did catch a cab and arrived, his appointment time was already past.

But now, none of that mattered because the Kifari had not failed to meet their appointment on time, and now the Review Board, his space base, and most of the Space Force no longer existed.

EMC (Earth Military Central) sent out the call for all survivors to report to a temporary HQ. Now Anders, who had never had sole control of a ship of any kind, let alone a Voidrunner class patrol ship, and who probably would have been kicked out of the Service, found himself a Brevet Captain in the Space Force.

Since Voidrunners used the Ego-Drive, they could only fly if they had people sitting in the Battery, powering the ship with their individual psychic energy. Each ship had to have a minimum of three psychic officers to serve the Battery in equal shifts. And the minimum was precisely what the *Restitution* had. Other than Anders, there were two ensigns: Ensign Arvin Chambers and Ensign Gary Laine. None of the three had awesome psychic potential, so more often than not, each put in a six-hour shift and the other six hours the ship just floated freely in space subject to the whim of solar winds.

The *Restitution*'s job was to patrol a very limited sector of space, one that the Brass considered an unlikely candidate for a Kifari invasion fleet. They were to watch and report, not attempt to engage. Despite its impressive sounding name, the *Restitution* wasn't going to gain vengeance on anybody. It had only light weaponry and almost no shielding. It was built to be stealthy and fast, not formidable.

Theirs would have been an easy job except for one thing—the crew!

The crew of the *Restitution* had been made up of the dregs of what were available after the Kifari assault. A few of the men had even been serving sentences in the brig. But after the attack, pardons were plentiful for those willing to swear their allegiance and promise to sin no more. Other members of the crew were relatively new recruits or those who had served the Space Force with the Quartermasters or clerical staff. The sad truth of the matter was that except for a couple of the men who had been biding their time in the brig, Anders had the most experience in space and that was next to nothing!

Now the *Restitution* had been on patrol for almost three months. Normally the patrol would almost be over, but with ships and crews at a premium, Anders' continued messages to Space Command had kept being put off with vague responses. There was no telling how long they might have to stay out in space and the men were beginning to grumble. A couple of them had even come down with what the medicos called *Voidphobia*, though the laymen simply referred to it as men getting *spacey*.

When a man got spacey, he tended to stare out into

nothing for long periods of time. His response time dropped radically and in extreme cases, some men had become suicidal. Anders knew he couldn't afford to let too many men get spacey. The inexperienced ones were bad enough but if many became ill, essential jobs wouldn't get done and then men might die. Anders figured his crew needed a diversion. It would be one thing if he could at least point to a definite date of return or at least furlough, but he had no such comfort to give them. Ensign Chambers had reported numerous small meetings of men clustered together talking in hushed voices when they should be busy at their duties.

So Capt. Anders made a command decision. He had desperately tried to avoid making decisions his entire career in the service. This time, he hoped he was making the right one.

Ensign Laine piped them to attention amidships. Capt. Anders couldn't help notice the sullen looks on many of their faces.

"Men, as you know, the Space Force has found it necessary to extend our tour of duty slightly and while we have plenty of food, it would probably be a good idea to replenish the raw materials that feed the converters that supply us with breathable air and water. While there are no Class M planets in our patrol sector, there are a number of large asteroids that might be able to provide us with the materials we need. We have spotted a few larger asteroids with what appear to be cores rich in nickel, iron, fosterite, and many other minerals. They also have ice mantles. What I am proposing is that we tie up to one of those asteroids and mine it for whatever we need. It will be hard work, but it will give you men a chance to get off-ship and stretch your legs. Therefore I had Ensign Chambers lay in a course to Asteroid J-119. I estimate we will arrive sometime tomorrow. Ensign

Laine will see you individually with your assignments. When we dock, the majority of you will suit up and get busy scavenging what you need. We'll keep a skeleton crew aboard ship at all times.

That night, Anders' sleep was disturbed by a timid knock at his cabin door. Wearily pushing the sleep from his eyes, Anders called out. "Permission to enter." Anders was even more annoyed when he saw who had disturbed his much needed rest. It was Seaman Quail. Of all the useless members of this crew, Quail was perhaps the most useless. He had been a Spaceman Recruit when he served in the typing pool on Earth Base Equator, and he had jumped at the opportunity for increasing his rank to Spaceman Apprentice after the disastrous attack. He had never even been into space before but here he was on the *Restitution*, and here he was keeping his captain from getting the rest he needed to rejuvenate his psychic talents, so recently drained by the Ego-Drive Battery.

Anders put on his stern-but-patient-face and sat up on his bunk. "Okay, Spaceman Quail, what could possibly be so important that you needed to wake me up instead of taking it up with one of the ensigns or almost anyone else as far as that goes?"

Normally this might have been enough to send Quail running for a place to hide in the hold, but this time Quail seemed to have some inner reserves of backbone and he stood to attention smartly. "Permission to close the door, Sir? What I have to say is of a highly secret nature."

Anders was intrigued. This seaman barely even sounded like the Quail he knew. He spoke with strength and confidence, two qualities that Quail had never even seemed to know. "Permission granted." Anders swung his legs over the edge of his bunk and pulled on his shoes without even knowing why. "Sit down, son."

Quail took the only chair in Anders' tiny cabin and pulled it over close to his captain. "First of all, Sir, I'd like you to take a moment and read this." Quail handed Anders a small sealed packet.

Anders broke the seal and started to read. "Wait. What? Is this true?"

"Sir, you can see that it is. My orders are very clear and now you know them."

What Anders was looking at left no room for doubt. He couldn't help but shake his head. "Why did you choose to make yourself known to me at this time? And why is a member of Space Military Intelligence aboard the *Restitution*?"

Quail's clear blue eyes locked on Anders' own. "Sir, I am not at liberty to answer your second question, but I will tell you why I have revealed myself to you, and it must be emphasized, only you. I am sure you and your other officers have been aware of quite a bit of grumbling from the men recently?"

"Sure. Spacemen always grumble. I think they must teach a course of it in Basic Training. What's your point, Quail?"

"This has been more than just the usual grumbling, Sir. The men led by Jenkins and Plano are planning to take over the ship once you resupply on Asteroid J-119. They plan to kill you and take the ensigns as prisoners to serve by keeping the battery charged. They mean to turn renegade or at least that's what they're telling the other men. I don't know if each and every man of the crew is in on this. I suspect the two spacey victims aren't anyway. Still there's going to be way too many for you and the ensigns to handle. Space Service isn't about to let any of our remaining vessels fall into the hands of the Kifari."

FINAL SHIPS IN THE NEIGHBORHOOD

Anders was stunned by what he was hearing. This mouse named Quail was actually a spy for SMI. He was telling Anders that the men were about to mutiny and take over his ship. "Wait, what was that last thing? Are you saying that Jenkins and Plano might be agents of the Kifari?"

"It's very possible, Sir. The Kifari attack on our base was way too accurate for it to have been happenstance. We are sure they had received inside information. So now we are keeping our eyes open for suspicious activities like these and others."

"I'll have them arrested and put in the brig until we return to Earth."

"Sir, with all due respect, you are not listening to what I am saying. Who would you order to arrest Jenkins and Plano? I know most of the crew is in on it but we don't know who is and isn't. If you give that order, it's more likely the ensigns will end up arrested and you'll wind up dead. No sir, we need to handle this in an entirely different way. They are not planning on making their move to take over the ship until we have all the raw materials aboard from the asteroid. So we just need to beat them to the punch."

"What do you mean, Quail?"

"It's really fairly simple, Sir. You go ahead and do just what you had told the men. Tether to the asteroid. Keep yourself, me, Corpsman Aims, the spacey victims, and one ensign on board as your skeleton crew. Land the rest of them on the asteroid with one of the ensigns in command. Tell the ensign he is to command the first shift of scavengers. While they are planetside, we'll make as many preparations as we can to untether and head back to Earth. When the ensign returns with the first load of materials, let them be brought aboard. As the landing party is returning to gather the second load, find some pretext to delay the ensign returning with them. Then we finish preparations, cut the tether, and return to Earth."

"Hold on, Mr. Quail! You expect me to maroon the majority of the crew on a lifeless asteroid? That's a death sentence! And we don't even know if all the men are guilty of wanting to mutiny. We certainly don't know that all of them are Kifari spies."

"And we probably never will know, Sir. But we're at war now and civilian niceties need not be observed. We've lost too many men and too many ships to the enemy already, and I'm not about to let them take one more. We need this ship and its officers way more than we need a small group of malcontents. May I remind you that some of these men might have already been responsible for the murders of tens of thousands of your brother officers and crewmen? This is the only possible course of action I see you having, Lt. Anders. You need to make a decision now. Tomorrow we'll be tethering to that asteroid. By the day after tomorrow, you might be dead and the *Restitution* might be in the hands of Kifari spies. So what are your orders, Sir?"

The next day, the *Restitution* arrived at J-119. The tetherplate was let out and made contact with the asteroid. Once again the men were piped to a meeting amidship.

"Men, we have arrived at J-119. Ensign Laine will be in charge of the landing party. I will stay on the *Restitution* with Ensign Chambers, Spaceman Quail, Corpsman Aims, and the two spacey victims, of course. Ensign Laine! After three hours you will bring a small party back with whatever raw materials you have gathered while the rest of the men keep mining. Then you will return and after three more hours, you'll bring the rest of what you have gathered and the men will rest. Tomorrow, we will follow the same procedure but Ensign

Chambers will lead the landing party. After six hours tomorrow, we should have enough to continue. While you and the men are mining, Ensign Chambers and I will continue to monitor the sector to make sure we are not surprised by any Kifari vessels. If we find any, we will call you and the entire party back to the ship and weigh anchor immediately. So stay at the ready! Men, suit up and gather your mining equipment and let's get busy!"

Fifteen minutes later the *Restitution* was down to a four-man crew and the two invalids. Anders gave Corpsman Aims orders to stay with the sick men. After Aims had gone belowdeck, Anders explained the situation to Ensign Chambers and they made ready for sudden departure. It took nearly the full three hours Anders had calculated it would with such reduced manpower.

Right on time, Ensign Laine came back with a five-man party, carrying the materials they had gathered thus far. After unloading the materials into the aft hold, Laine prepared to return to the digging site with the five men.

"Ensign Laine, I need you to stay here a little while and look at a communiqué I intend to send to Central Command and give me your opinion. Send the men back to the digging site and you can follow them shortly."

After the men had gone, Capt. Anders gave Laine a very brief rundown of the situation, putting final touches on the takeoff procedure. Anders himself released the tetherplate and the *Restitution* started to drift away from J-119. When a safe distance had been reached, the engines roared to life. Almost immediately frantic messages came in from the helmet coms of the men on the asteroid trying to ascertain what was going on. Anders ignored them and shortly, there was no way the would-be mutineers could get back on to the ship.

73

FINAL SHIPS IN THE NEIGHBORHOOD

The men's questions turned to screams and pleas for mercy over the radio. Soon, the *Restitution* was too far away for such short-range communications.

Spaceman Quail stood on deck with Brevet Captain Anders.

Quail spoke quietly to Anders. "I know that couldn't have been an easy order for you to give, Captain, to leave the majority of your crew on that desolate rock. Sentencing them to certain death takes a certain kind of steel in a man, which I wasn't sure you had. I was allowed to read your file when they assigned me as an Undercover on this ship. Obviously they had you all wrong. The file indicated you were timid and uncertain and might not be able to command effectively in life and death situations."

Anders turned away from Quail so the anguish on his face would not show. "No Quail, they had me right in that folder. That was the toughest thing I ever had to do, but I knew I HAD to do it for myself, for the Service and for Earth. I'll probably see those men in my nightmares for the rest of my life. My only hope is that the Service doesn't court-martial or execute me for the decision I made here today."

Quail walked around Anders and looked him straight in the eyes. "I assure you after I file my report with Intelligence, the Service will view the death of the crew as acceptable losses in a military necessity."

There was a catch in Anders' throat as he repeated, "Acceptable losses! But acceptable to whom?"

An Afterword to this story is on page 203.

8

THE SHOOTING STAR

by
Gail Harkins

"Jesse! Where are the car keys? I need them now!" Tatiana rummaged through the kitchen drawer that normally stored the family's key rings.

"What's the rush?" Her teenaged brother swept his black hair across his forehead and leaned against the center island.

"I'm late for my fitting..."

"Oh yeah." He removed the key ring from his leather jacket pocket. "I don't know what you see in that rich dude anyway. It's not like he's fun or anything."

She snatched the keys from his hand and dashed out the door to the old Volvo parked in the drive. Easing it into gear, she backed into the street. After sitting interminably at two red lights, she used the time at the third traffic light to phone the bridal shop.

"I'm on my way. Traffic's heavy. I should be there in about 15 minutes."

"That's fine. Thank you for phon—Ahhh!"

A scream and the whoosh of an explosion pierced the air. Brown smoke rose above the buildings in the direction of the shop. Tatiana drove as close as she could, then walked through the crowds that had gathered on the sidewalks to gape as flames devoured the buildings.

"What happened?" she asked, moving forward slowly.

"I don't know...an explosion...maybe a gas leak..." The answers varied but a conclusion was expected. Lives were lost, much of the block was destroyed, and her wedding dress, with its satin skirt and French lace bodice, was toast, just as she would have been if Jesse hadn't pocketed the car keys.

* * *

"It's a sign." Her best friend, Julie, was adamant. "I tell you, you're not meant to marry that man!"

Waiters bustled past, serving lunch to a clientele buzzing with speculation about that morning's explosion. Through the windows, they watched smoke rising from the wreckage.

"His name's Adam. And, he's perfectly...nice." Tatiana glared and sipped her tea.

Julie rolled her eyes. "Nice. 'He's perfectly nice.' So where's the passion? Where's the *we-were-meant-to-be-together, love-of-a-lifetime, soul-mate, other-half-of-me* passion?"

"Like you and Jim? Not everybody's like that. Adam's sweet and caring and will take care of Jesse and me." But in her heart, she yearned for the head-over-heels, lasso-the-moon-love that Julie and Jim shared.

When Adam came to her house that evening, he was solicitous. "I brought pizza. After what happened at the bridal shop today, I thought you might not want to go out to dinner."

FINAL SHIPS IN THE NEIGHBORHOOD

Jesse breezed into the room and spied the pizza boxes. "Cool! Can I take one to Connor's?"

Adam handed him the top box.

"Thanks!" Jesse called as the screen door slammed.

"How'd you know?" Tatiana asked.

Adam grinned. "I used to be a teenager. They're bottomless pits."

"Well, it was kind of you."

They ate their dinner in front of the TV, as the evening news played clips of the fiery explosion and firefighters' efforts to contain the blaze.

He hugged her tightly. "It frightens me to think I could have lost you in that inferno."

Tatiana was shaken, too. "Thanks to a happy accident, I wasn't."

Adam gathered their plates and Tatiana took the leftover pizza to the kitchen. He steered her back to the living room. "Wait here. I have a surprise for you."

When he returned with a large dress box, faded from decades of storage, Tatiana felt her chest tighten in trepidation.

"Your wedding dress was destroyed in the explosion, and there's only two weeks before the wedding. So I hope you don't mind...I brought you my mother's wedding gown. I told her what happened and she said of course you should have it."

Tatiana inhaled deeply. "It's...sweet of her...and you," she quickly added as her heart plummeted to her stomach. She left the box on the table where he had placed it.

"Don't you want to see it?" he prompted.

"After you leave. It's bad luck for the groom to see the gown before the wedding."

FINAL SHIPS IN THE NEIGHBORHOOD
* * *

She waited until Julie arrived to open the box. "Adam's mom was an actress before she married," she confided, carefully removing the gown from its tissues.

"She was rather…fashion forward…wasn't she?" Julie asked, spreading the satin folds over the bed. "Are you sure this is a wedding gown?"

The neckline plunged in a deep "V" that stopped just above the navel, barely a hand span before the side slit began.

"Maybe there's a jacket somewhere…" Tatiana said hopefully, rummaging through the tissue. She sighed deeply. "Julie, I can't wear this! I'd look like a space-alien hooker! How can I tell Adam? He's been so…"

"Nice," Julie finished for her. "He's always 'nice.'"

When Adam rang the next morning, he was apologetic. "Mother says I only brought one of the boxes. I'll bring the other by this evening and we can go out to dinner."

"Adam, you don't have to—"

"Don't be silly. I want to."

She met him at the door. "Adam, really, this is too much to ask."

"But you're not asking. " He put the box on the dining table. "You must have had quite a fright when you opened the box."

She relaxed visibly. "Then you understand."

"Of course. You can't accessorize a divine dress like that nowadays. That's why Mother insisted on this." He opened the box and Julie gasped.

"You'll be just as beautiful as Mother." He cocked his head in appraisal. "You know, with your hair that way, you look exactly like her at your age."

Alone in her room that night, she leaned against the bed pillows, talking to herself. "He's a good man. A kind man. This is just an aberration. It's just a dress. He loves me. He cares for Jesse, too. It's just a dress." She sobbed. "An ugly, trashy, tarted up dress that he wants me to wear on the most important day of my life!"

* * *

She met Julie the next day at a bistro near her office. They sat at a small table with a view of the cherry trees across the street in the park. In another week, they would be in bloom.

"I'd say it can't be that bad, but I saw the dress!" her friend said, then sipped her tea. "Maybe you can spill something on it. Have some red wine when you show it to me again and I'll do the deed."

"I'll keep your offer in mind," Tatiana replied. "Right now, I'm more concerned about his relationship with his mother."

"Umm." She nodded, taking a bite. "Mamma's boy. If you marry him, she'll run his life and yours, too."

Tatiana frowned. "I just don't understand how this could be."

"The signs have always been there. You just ignored them."

Tatiana's scowl deepened as she picked at her croissant.

"Think about it. When you went skiing, his mom came along."

"She had friends in Aspen."

"Your evening at the ballet?"

"It was the Bolshoi's last performance on the tour."

Julie grimaced. "Well then, think about your birthday present. His mother picked it out! And that rock on your finger? You told me that his mother previewed rings with him. Face it, sweetie. Your man's tied to momma's apron strings!"

Tatiana hated to admit it, but Julie was right. She'd seen the signs, and she'd dismissed them, pushed each one to the back of her mind and shut the figurative door. But, she told herself, there were worse things than being married to a man who loved his mother.

She poured over pattern books and bridal magazines that afternoon, and finally took the wedding gown to a seamstress.

"Ooh la la! Your mother-in-law was a live one!" the woman exclaimed when she saw the dress. "What do you have in mind, honey?"

Tatiana handed her a folder and tapped a photograph of an elegant, figure-skimming gown. "This was the gown I chose, but it went up in smoke in the explosion." She tapped another photo. "Could you maybe make something like this out of the gown?"

The seamstress looked at the photo and at the gown. "I can add some fabric here and fill in the slit with a pleat." She nodded. "Yes. I'll make you a beautiful gown for your wedding day."

The seamstress worked swiftly and soon Tatiana returned for a fitting. Julie met her there.

"Amazing! I'd never guess it was the same gown if I didn't know. Now you look like a princess," Julie pronounced.

They left separately, Julie to return to work, and Tatiana to meet Adam at the caterers. Tatiana was at the point where the highway hugged the river when the engine died. As the car coasted, she tried repeatedly to restart the engine, crossing traffic lanes gingerly to reach the side of the highway. Safely there, she turned the key again and again. The engine was silent. The next move was to call Adam and a tow truck.

Reaching into her purse, she felt for her cell phone, and then remembered. She had plugged it in to charge. It was still on the bureau at home. "The one time I really need it!" she fumed.

When she finally reached her house, her cell phone had five messages from Adam.

"What happened? You were supposed to meet me at the caterer's and then you didn't answer your phone," he began.

"It's a long story. The car died and I didn't have my phone. I had to walk to the next exit ramp and find a pay phone. Do you know how hard it is to find a pay phone nowadays? And get a tow truck and wait for a cab? I ran out of change before I could phone you. I just got home and I'm exhausted."

"My poor darling," he tut-tutted. "I'm glad you're all right. Take a hot bath and get some dinner. Order in. I'll talk to you tomorrow. Oh, I took care of the caterer. We had to change the menu. We're having veal."

"No we're not. No way. Do you really understand what that is? Not intellectually, but really understand? I'll change it back tomorrow."

She hung up and phoned Julie.

"You sound like you had a rough day," her friend said when she hear Tatiana's voice.

"You don't know the half of it!" Tatiana replied and proceeded to itemize the many ways it had gone wrong.

"It's a sign. You're not supposed to marry Adam."

"Nonsense. People have car trouble all the time."

"Name the last time you had car trouble."

She played with her hair with one hand and held the phone with the other. "I can't."

"See? It's a sign. I'm telling you, the universe does not

want you to marry this guy."

"His name's Adam. And the universe has nothing to do with it."

"Suit yourself."

* * *

Tatiana shared Julie's perspective with Adam a few days later as they walked the path along the canal that connected the city with the sea. A large yacht, the *Shooting Star*, slowly sailed past, its sails stately in the morning light. Adam followed it with his eyes, then returned his attention to his fiancée.

"That's ridiculous!" His eyes crinkled as he scoffed.

"That's what I told her, but what if she's right? What if these are signs telling us we really shouldn't marry?"

"Then I would have gotten signs, too, and nothing bad's happened to me." He put his arm around her and kissed the top of her head. "You just have pre-wedding jitters."

"Adam?"

"Yes?"

"Nothing…"

* * *

The wedding ceremony was scheduled to begin at 10:00 a.m. in the same downtown church in which Adam's parents were married.

Julie was driving Tatiana there along streets lined with cherry trees just turning pink. The wedding gown lay across the back seat. Suddenly, she pulled the car to the side of the road.

"What are you doing?" Tatiana asked.

FINAL SHIPS IN THE NEIGHBORHOOD

Julie pointed. "There." A white contrail arced across the cloudless sky behind a brilliant fireball.

"A missile?"

"I don't think so." Julie squinted into the glare. "Maybe a meteor? But that's impossible."

"No. Just improbable."

They watched, mesmerized, as it approached. The shock wave, when it came, thudded through them. The sound was like thunder. When they reached the church, the stained glass had been blown inward, littering the pews and shredding the flowers adorning the altar.

Tatiana's heart was still racing as she walked through the damaged sanctuary. She surveyed the scene through blank eyes and turned to Julie. "A gas explosion destroyed the bridal shop, my car died going to the caterer's, and a meteor exploded over the church. One is bad luck. Two is coincidence. Three has to be some kind of sign." She shook her head, disbelieving the evidence around her. "I'm cursed. That's it. I'm cursed."

Outside, car alarms still sounded and people were shouting.

"It should have been such a perfect day." She looked around the now-tattered church again as tears formed.

"Tatiana! Julie!"

The women turned to a figure breaking through the knot of people and into the church.

"Adam!"

He ran to them and wrapped his arms around his bride-to-be. "Thank goodness you're safe. I must be the luckiest man alive. When I saw your car and saw the church..." He kissed her passionately, fiercely, as if their entire lives were wrapped into that single moment.

For Tatiana, time seemed to stop. The world fell away. The church, the shards of glass, and the people gawking at the damage all disappeared. For this moment, there was only Adam. She felt the rumble in her soul as she realized that in his arms, she was at home. The electricity built. The frisson of excitement reached her very toes. The air around them seemed to hum with possibilities.

"I want to marry you now," he told her. "Today, just as planned."

"I love you too, desperately," she admitted, as she realized she did love Adam, truly, deeply, and far more than she imagined. Her jitters of the past few weeks had been just that, and nothing more. "But, we can't. The church..." She spread her hands.

"We can. There's a ship in town and I know the captain."

The corners of her lips lifted in a bemused grin. "Your mother?"

"It's her ship and her captain. We can be married at sea."

* * *

The *Shooting Star* left port that morning, bound for the open ocean with the wedding party on board.

The teak deck was decorated with flowers Julie had salvaged from the ruined church. The schooner changed course and adjusted its sails to go wing-on-wing. With the main sail and jib on opposite sides of the vessel and the wind directly behind the beam, the wind seemed to die and the *Shooting Star* felt as if it floated on air, although it still cut through the sea at a fast pace.

Tatiana stepped on deck in her mother-in-law's wedding gown, which had been remade into an elegant creation with a drapeau neckline.

Adam's mother gasped when she saw her. "That's not my wedding dress!" she whispered. Her voice trailed off. "That's the costume I wore in *Maid of Mars*."

Tatiana's shoulders trembled in suppressed laughter.

Her soon-to-be mother-in-law smiled. "You look beautiful, my dear!"

Tatiana walked to the center of the deck, where Adam took her hands in his own. Before the captain and the assembled company, the couple promised to love and to cherish each other from this day forth. As Adam slipped the wedding band on her finger, two white contrails arced across the sky behind brilliant fireballs.

Julie's voice rang from the crowd, "Three meteors in one day! This is definitely a sign!"

An Afterword to this story is on page 204.

9

DRAGON SHIP

by
Andy McKell

The storm had battered the Castle on the Rock for days without end, lashing the ancient walls with a fury unknown in living memory. Once-proud royal banners hung in tatters from the towers. No patrols rode the paths or borders, and battlement guards hid in their turrets. There would be no patrols to greet, no travelers seeking shelter, no enemy insane enough to attack in this blinding rain.

The dying king, seated in a great chair and wrapped in winter furs against the biting cold, leaned closer to the fire in his private chambers. He held up the palms of his withered hands to capture the warmth of the flames and rubbed them together slowly, to stimulate some inner fire. The only sounds were the crackling of the logs and the howling of the wind outside, hammering against the stout walls and seeking to gain entry.

As if speaking out loud in the conclusion of a long,

thoughtful inner debate, he spoke without turning from the fire, "You see, Meacham, the old days are behind us."

Standing beside him was a younger man, tall and straight-backed, who was becoming used to strange utterances from the king who had once been a mighty warrior, but who was sliding into decline in the personal winter of his years. "The past, Sire, is a certainty."

The king turned his head painfully and fixed the gaze of his remaining eye on the one man he had trusted as adviser these many years. He stared for a long time, the firelight glittering on the watery surface of that weeping eye, before scolding his companion. "You need not humor me, Meacham. I am talking about the turning of the years, the changing of the ways.

"When our forefathers fell from the sky and found themselves in this accursed land, they did not whimper and cower. No! They strode out across the lands, driving back the wargs and the boreas and the other horrid creatures, destroying the poisonous plants, building strong dwellings, farms, cities...they did not mewl like babes-in-arms, as do these new men. No! They were made of different stuff.

"The old days, the old ways, are behind us. We must try to survive and prosper with men of bronze, instead of the golden heroes of the past." He sighed heavily and again fell silent for a long period.

His companion waited patiently, gazing into the leaping flames and thinking his thoughts.

"So, Meacham, you have known all of these new men, these boys, their entire lives, although how you have maintained the appearance of youth over such a time remains a mystery to me. Perhaps you could share it with me before it is too late?"

"Sire, I am what I am, fortunate or cursed, it is not for me to say." There was a trace of bitterness in his voice, but the king was too distracted to notice. How he longed to give this good man the longevity his own people took as a right. But it was forbidden.

The old man sighed heavily. "Same old Meacham. I have been grateful for the secrets of mine you have kept close over the years, so I should not begrudge you one of your own. Very well, back to the point. Which of the whimpering pups and soft-bellied wastrels who court my favor shall win the prize? To whom can I safely entrust my people, the Baxtersland, the future?"

"Sire, if you demand the truth, I must say—at risk to your health—Simeon."

The king raged. "That name is forbidden. I send him out to subdue the eastern barbarian tribes, and the fool goes and marries one of their princesses!"

"It would be to seal a peace, to unite the peoples, Sire."

"So you say. But what does he say, eh? Nothing! And when I call him to me to explain himself, he ignores my summons. If my own son cannot come when called…" His voice broke up into a fit of coughing.

"Sire, we do not know if he even received the call. The storms are making travel hazardous. We do not know if he is facing attack from the eastern tribes or if pestilence has struck. There are reports of the oceans rising as mountains along the coasts. There is widespread destruction. There are many good reasons why he could not come."

The king spoke, almost to himself. "Yes, the world

does appear to be collapsing upon us. Is it a punishment for my indecision?"

"The storms predate your recent illness, Sire."

"Ever tactful, my good friend. I am not ill.; I am dying. But you can see far, I know you can. Can you see him?" His voice rose in hope.

"I cannot see into the hearts of men as far away as the eastern lands, Sire."

"Then what good are you to me?" The king's mood had swung again. He gestured angrily, a weak, dismissive motion. "Name me another. Simeon is no longer my son. His appointment as my heir is cancelled. There must be another."

"But I have no name to give to you, other than the one I am forbidden to speak. However, we should consider your nephew, Berring—"

"That weaver of schemes and plots? He only lives still due to my love of my sister, blessed may she rest in the realm of Heaven's Eye, from which we fell." He did not hurry the ritual phrase. He meant every word.

"Sire, if he is not made king, he will challenge whoever is enthroned. War is inevitable."

"I know that well, Meacham." He closed his eye and held still for a long time until Meacham thought he had fallen asleep. Then the king spoke quietly as if to himself. "I often wished I had it in me to remove him from the game. But I cannot do that."

Was the king asking Meacham to do what he could not bring himself to do? Was he asking for someone to rid him of this troublesome nephew? He suppressed his pain. He could not provide this service to a king and a people he had come to love. It was forbidden.

Instead, Meacham continued his analysis of Berring. "Other than…" He drew himself up short. "He is the only one strong enough to hold the Kingdom together, but it will be with the sword."

"Of the lesser candidates, a man often grows to fill the position he is given. If he does not, then someone more able will step forward and replace him." Meacham spoke as if from experience. "But there will be little time to grow into a position to stand against Berring."

"War if I choose Berring, war if I don't?" The king stirred with a shadow of his former passion. "Replacement? By assassination? Civil war? I will not leave warfare as my legacy. D'ye hear me? I am the Rock to my people. I want a name." A hand, white as snow, feebly grasped Meacham's robe in desperation.

Meacham considered the dark veins as thin as sewing cotton that ran between the many brown blotches of aging on the king's hand. He shuddered at these signs of a mortality he would not himself face until the king's far descendents squatted amid the ruins of these lands, trying to remember how to make fire.

"C'mon, I don't have long and I need a name. Surely, there is one man worthy of the title? Someone you can groom, perhaps? Someone who can stand against Berring, with you at his side?" The distress on his face was reflected in his wavering voice. It was painful to hear. "My loyal friend, you can train one, another one, advise him…" The one eye twinkled as if sharing a secret. "Even tell him what to do, as you have me these past decades. C'mon, don't deny it." The old man's chuckle was feeble. He was losing strength quickly."

"Sire, I must deny anything but speaking true to my king. But it takes time to…groom a king. The lands do not have time to grow a strong king to whom Berring would submit."

"Again…war if I choose him and war if I don't."

After a moment, the king's mood changed. His voice rose. "In other times, I would castrate and cast out the lot of them, nephews, cousins, all of them." His rising anger distressed him. Again, he broke up in a fit of coughing.

Meacham lifted a beaker of water to his king's lips, smiling at the unspoken gratitude in that one, watery eye. Before long, the king slipped into a deep, restful sleep. There was more than water in that beaker. Meacham wished he could do more, but it was forbidden. He adjusted the fur coverings and summoned royal guards to watch over the king. He could not trust any other person in this entire world. There was too much at stake.

* * *

Night deepened at the western stronghold, then slowly passed away into the memory of dreams.

Far to the east, the first light of breaking dawn touched the strong face of the king's son, Simeon standing alone on the battlements of the fortress guarding against the barbarian hordes.

* * *

Heaven's Eye eased itself above the dark storm-clouds gathering on the Eastern Ocean's distant horizon, casting its deep red glow on a day renewed. The expected attack had not come. The skies had not burned with fire launched at the lands, not this night. Perhaps the next one, or the one after that?

The land had shaken again as if great giants had fallen. Riders had taken their chances and hurried with news of great upheavals of the oceans, far to the north and south. At least the lands around had been spared that disaster, so far. But with fields and orchards flooded, cattle stranded or washed away, he had no clue as to how long the castle folk and the never-ending flow of refugees would survive.

For this brief moment, however, it seemed to Simeon that every living thing in the eastern lands had breathed a collective sigh of relief at surviving the night. Deep inside, he knew these were merely the normal morning habits of the natural world.

Avians shook off the night's torpor, each broadcasting its personal song of joy. In every place where darkness was dispelled, creatures stirred, their simple thoughts turning to breakfast. But it was thus every day. Simeon was projecting his relief onto the world around him.

He gazed out at the lands from atop the high battlements and thought himself pleased to be alive. They had survived the night. But how many nights remained before the great fire would be launched?

At least the raging storms had abated for a brief spell this morning, although he knew what weather was rolling in rapidly from the east.

Simeon knew the Dragon Ship was up there,

somewhere above those clouds, but over which land it floated, he could not guess. Or was it over the ocean that stretched to the daily rebirthing-place of Heaven's Eye? Some of the sailors who had survived the destruction claimed the ship could rise to the very stars. Nonsense, of course. Nevertheless, this was a ship that sailed not upon the waves but upon the clouds, a ship that floated not in water, but in air. How was that possible? And if that were possible, then why not a ship that could rise to the stars?

"You need to sleep, my Lord."

He had not heard the approaching footsteps of his steward. He was exhausted; he had to admit. He spoke without turning. "Thank you, Andreo, but I know that. Please tell me something I do not know, but only tell me something good."

Before his steward could speak, there came the steady, measured paces of a man biding his time, although Simeon knew of his cousin's growing impatience. Still gazing out across the ocean, watching the gathering storm clouds, Simeon whispered, "That sound does not signal the approach of good news."

His mood fell as dark as the rain-heavy sky fast approaching. He turned to face his cousin. "Good morning, Berring. And how does Heaven's Eye find you today?"

"As ever, it looks and sees. That is how it finds me."

Simeon smiled, shaking his head in disbelief. "And *as ever*, you are too literal. Is there still no trace of poetry in your soul?"

"My loyalty belongs to the throne. My duty belongs to you. My soul belongs to Heaven's Eye, from which we fell." He ended the ritual on a note of finality, dismissing further discussion of poetry and souls. "I note that the famous Ship of the Skies did not come like a dragon, spouting fire."

"Are you denying that half our fleet is destroyed, Berring? We have witness reports from those who survived the attacks."

"Does my Lord fear the tales of ignorant fishermen, who seek to justify the loss of their boats? Or gold-palming pirates we deem to call merchants? Or cowardly sailors who abandoned the ships of the Kingdom's fleet for no good reason? Dragon Ships? Pah! If you would allow me to question—"

"You mean torture."

"To *question* these men, I am sure I shall cut through their childish fantasies and get to the truth."

"My decision stands." He stood firm, to assert his authority against his cousin's challenge.

"Then I shall see you at breakfast and every other breakfast until these delusions are scattered like the marsh-mists they are." He gathered his black cloak around him, nodded to his Lord, and strode away, his pace not quite as measured and not quite as patient as when he arrived.

Simeon and Andreo watched him in silence as he departed.

The Lord finally spoke his thoughts. "What if my cousin is correct? I do sometimes wonder at these tales of great, black hulls appearing from the worst of the storms, riding on towers of fire, seeking to destroy us.

"If not an attack, then simply a careless and casual destruction? If a ship that sails the skies does truly float on clouds, perhaps the storms that destroyed our vessels were caused by its disturbance of the clouds it travels on? Perhaps these storms are just an accident?"

"It matters not, Sire. Yes, our fleet is lost, but such a fleet could do nothing against the Ship of the Skies. Our ships' prow-rams can only batter what stands on the waters. Our arrows cannot reach the sky. Our swords are useless against an enemy that will not stand and place its own warriors' bodies at risk. They ignore our attempts to signal them to parley. There is nothing to be done. We can only wait for the crew of the Dragon Ship to do what they will do, be it launching fire from the sky, or bringing more storms--even if that is by accident."

"Andreo, you say our fate lies in the hands of those who sail the skies. Could this be true? That a man can do nothing? His life and dreams all coming to nothing at the whim of unknown people? Could our destruction be caused by the actions of powerful folk who simply disregard us? If you are correct, then the sky-people are truly not human and we are powerless. They have no hearts. How can we ever understand such people?"

* * *

"Empyrean Sir, the situation is becoming critical in the Baxtersland zone. Satellite observation shows the disruption of weather systems continues to worsen across the planet. Tectonic plate damage is launching massive tsunamis across the coasts."

"Your orders stand. The ocean mining operations will continue until the ore is depleted. In time, the climate will recover. Your claims for compensation or evacuation are rejected. Yes, these people are a

lost colony from the Great Expansion, but they are degenerates. Too primitive to understand the wider implications of civilization and the Empire. Not ready for incorporation, if they ever will be. And it's not our job. We are not the Colonial Service."

"Understood, Empyrean Sir. But it is difficult to stand by and watch such widespread suffering—"

"Do not tell me you have gone native, Resident? Remember, you can be replaced as easily as your predecessors in the Meacham role."

"I understand, Empyrean Sir. I simply ask you to reconsider the schedule for an end to mining operations."

"The Empire hears you, again. The Empire rejects your request, again. Contact terminated."

* * *

Berring stood by the fireplace in his chambers, the flickering flames the only illumination. From the collection of intercepted messages between king and son, he selected the rolled scroll bearing the king's summons to his son. It could be used as evidence of a disloyal son, when the time came. Or it could prove evidence of his manoeuvrings and treachery. He weighed the parchment in his hand, trying to decide whether it should be destroyed or preserved.

"A gesture of my hand and the document is gone. It is such a small thing, a feathersweight. Strange how destiny is weighed in the balance so lightly. Its future is decided so carelessly."

There was, after all, a poetry in his soul--the poetry of power.

* * *

FINAL SHIPS IN THE NEIGHBORHOOD

Far to the west, Meacham stood at the rain-lashed window of his chamber. Meacham, the latest in a long series of advisers to the king, each one cosmetically altered to appear to be the same man. Meacham, resident agent for a sprawling, impersonal galaxy-spanning Empire, forged by humanity over millennia. To the Empire, this planet was just another rock to plunder. He knew he was watching a world fall into ruin through greed above and ambition below. And he knew he was powerless.

In the king's chambers, an old man slipped the chains of life. The anguish of leadership and the future of his people now lay in other hands. It no longer mattered whose.

An Afterword to this story is on page 205.

10

THE MUD RACE

by
H.M. Schuldt

At any moment, the fourth meteor strike is going to begin hitting North and South America. I have been struggling with doubts about where I am and what I am doing with my life ever since the third meteor strike in May. The third strike caused the most damage, wiping out more than half the people, animals, and ships on Earth, yet somehow I know this is all meant to be. To some degree, we are all thinking it: *Will I survive the next strike?*

We are somewhere on the west side of North Carolina, and it is my first time going to the mudflats to see a race. It is Piper's first time, too. Piper never assures me of my safety because his focus is on a successful outcome. *Can he really pull this off—win the purse and drive away with his truck undamaged? He's rather ambitious.* I fold the corner of the page I had been reading and set my book next to my left leg in the passenger seat, *Women's Rights In Another Galaxy*. Piper drives his white Jeep Wrangler into the parking lot and looks for Vinny.

A black Jeep pulls into a parking spot, and Piper steps over to greet his racing buddy, Vinny Briscoe, and Vinny's girlfriend, Stella. They get out of Vinny's Jeep. I had met her at the movie theater last spring when she was with Vinny.

"Vinny!" she cries out in the parking lot. "My ticket!"

Vinny reaches into his pocket, hands her a little paper stub, and looks proud. "Don't say I neva' did nothin'."

Piper and Vinny get back in their trucks and enter through the gate as racers. Stella and I head to the entrance as spectators.

Stella speaks with a New York accent. "What a nice surprise, Linda. Vinny neva said nothin about you comin' along with Pipa. I came out ta see the *mystery ship* everyone's talkin' about. You know, it just happened to show up in the mudflats. I mean, how'd it do that? I've got to see it with my own eyes to believe it."

"I wonder how it got there." It's hard to get my mind wrapped around the fact that somehow the ship showed up in a muddy place.

How can it ever be the same? The meteor strikes have ruined the Earth. What is this world coming to? And how can the cost of living still be the same? It's been in the news non-stop ever since the third meteor strike. Other storms have made things move around, but this ship is a fish out of water.

"It's been fun keeping in contact with you and Vinny and Piper on social media. When Piper told me he registered for a mud race, I didn't even know that these things existed. Yesterday, he invited me to come along. It was a last minute thing. You know, the third strike…it really shook me up."

"Hey girl, it shook everyone up, even the whole planet."

With a deep consciousness of how this race has become the most important event to Piper, added to the fact that he has no interest in joining his father's motorcycle business, I begin to receive a revelation of perseverance, passion, and goals. These qualities in Piper impress me especially since they are missing in my life. My only determination, passion, and goals, as it would seem, apply to finishing a good book.

What am I doing here? I should have stayed back home where I could be drinking iced tea and reading my book in a comfortable chair. Why is this mystery ship so important? Don't people care about the next meteor strike due to hit Earth at any moment?

People crowd around at the entrance. There are all kinds of signs sticking up from the ground on wood sticks. NO GLASS BOTTLES. GATES OPEN AT 8AM. TRUCKS ONLY. NO DIRTBIKES. NO ATVS. GOLF CARTS WELCOME ON TRAILS ONLY. CAMPING FRI & SAT NIGHT. NO PETS. ENTER AT YOUR OWN RISK. FIRES IN BARRELS ONLY. NO THROWING ROCKS. NO FIGHTING. SPECTATORS MUST STAY BEHIND THE FENCE. SPINNING IN MUD PITS ONLY. VIOLATORS WILL BE REMOVED.

As a *walk-up*, I pay twenty-five dollars to get in. It had been a last minute decision to go to the races with Piper, so I missed the early bird discount of twenty dollars. The lady hands me a map and tells me to have a good time. Not knowing what to expect, I begin to doubt that I will have a good time. What could be so fun about watching trucks drive around and around when half the world is gone? *My mother is right. I need to do something more important with my life. Why did I ever come out here? Where did Stella go? Did I lose her?* I look around and see her standing by herself while she fidgets with her map.

"Linda…" Stella takes a quick glance to notice I am standing with her. She squints as she brings the map closer to her. "Why do they have to make it so difficult? It doesn't even say where ta go!"

"It's Cylinda, not Linda."

"Yeah. Well, you know. I'm terrible with names. It sounds like *Linda*, and you sort'a look like a *Linda*." Her tone is husky and honest.

"Well, it's *Cylinda*. Sort of like Cinderella." I open up my map to find the nearest restroom. "My mom wanted to name me Cinderella, but my dad wouldn't go for it. He thought I'd get teased, and people would ask to see my glass slippers, so they settled on Cylinda."

"Cinderella—kinda catchy. Why would anyone tease *you*? You'd neva hurt a flea."

"Never mind." I don't think it is necessary to refer to the glass slipper, so I change the subject. "I've never been to a mud race before."

"Me eith'a. Piper made you pay? Ugh!" Her jaw dropped open, and she frowned. Her right arm pulled up into the air, and she gave me a friendly slug in my left shoulder. "Tsa! Don't let him get away with it."

Ow! That really hurt! I rub it out to get rid of the pain.

A couple of teenage boys walk by and smirk. "You girls lost already?"

"Oh, get a life." Stella's natural tendency was defensiveness. "Go both'a someone else." If there is one thing Stella could do, she could stick up for herself. The first time we met, it was at the movie theater. Piper and I met up with her and Vinny at the Cinema Six several months ago when the first meteor strike hit in March. Stella ended up getting into an argument with the concession-stand cashier, and she demanded to get free tickets for bad customer service. Since the cashier didn't ring her up for the *popcorn special*, she claimed he had purposefully ripped her off by charging her the regular price for a large popcorn, candy, and soda. Stella turned it into a big scene. We ended up seeing *Prison Island*, a thriller where one of the inmates thinks he's a doctor sent there to help the other inmates. After the movie had ended, we learned that the first meteor strike had started to hit parts of Europe and Asia and would continue to strike down, over several days, landing on Earth in random locations. That's when strange things began to happen.

* * *

"You shoulda' given me the *popcorn special*! What, are you ripping me off now? I WANNA SEE THE MANAGER!"

When the manager finally came around, he apologized and gave her two free tickets to come back and see another movie.

"But you ruined my night, and I'm with my friends. We need four tickets to make it even."

The manager handed two more tickets to Stella.

"But she didn't ask for the *special*." I heard the cashier speak to the manager.

"The customer's always right! You oughta' know betta!" Stella's act of disapproval ended as we began to walk away with free tickets. She flashed the free tickets at me, lifted her eyebrows, and grinned behind the manager's back.

Stella is someone who I don't want to get on her bad side. It is a nice feeling to have someone sticking up for us, but I felt embarrassed about what we had to go through. The four of us returned the next month with four free tickets. We saw *The Unexpected Suspect*, a thriller about a girl, Norma, who goes out on a blind date with a new friend, Jessica, and two strange boys. One of the boys is murdered, and Norma is accused of the crime. At the very end, Norma discovers the unlikely suspect. We saw this movie when the second meteor strike hit Earth during the last week in April. News reports said that the destruction was minimal and some buildings had been wiped out. Other conflicting reports said that whole buildings had vanished.

* * *

"I don't mind paying for my own ticket." I look up from the map. "I don't want to feel like I owe Piper anything. We're just friends."

"Well, don't give him any gas money, girlfriend. Where do we go, anyway?"

"This place is bigger than Disneyland. It looks like the track for the first round is the small one." I bring my eyes up from the map and point to the left. I briefly think about how it's terrible that Disneyland and Disney World were wiped out by the third meteor strike in May. "Looks like the mystery ship is over by the first track. It's that way. We go to the Sticky Stand. I need to use the restroom first."

Stella decides she is also going to empty her *bladdah*. While sitting on the toilet, I notice the door in front of me. There is a poster hanging on the door with a big picture of a butterfly. It's beautiful. After relieving myself, I walk over to wash my hands. The automatic soap dispenser spits a brown substance in my hand. When I place my hands under the faucet, water streams out automatically. The soap begins to feel slippery as I mix it around on my palms. *Is this some kind of muddy soap? Weird.* I rinse my hands and while I am drying them with a paper towel, I notice many posters hanging on the wall: FROGS! DONATE TODAY! *Look at how many animals are endangered! How do we know what they're going to do with the money?* 'How do they know all these animals are endangered?"

"They research it, girlfriend." Stella dries her hands while standing next to me. She speaks confidently as if she has the frog situation figured out.

Her arms are moving, and it makes me think about protecting my shoulder. I take a step away, in case she decides to give me another one of her slugs.

"Awe. They're so cute." Stella likes the frog poster.

I notice big black bulging eyes and a shiny wet nose designed on the poster. It is not possible for me to imagine the frog as *cute*. "Cute?"

"Someone's gotta save 'em. I'll give em' a dolla'. Where do we go to give 'em a dolla'?"

"Oh, look. It says the St. Francis Butterfly is also endangered. They take donations at the Mud Market."

When we arrive at the Sticky Stand, which is nothing more than the type of metal bleachers at a high school football game, Stella shows great enthusiasm to see that the last two seats available are down in the front row.

"How lucky can we get? The best seats in the house, huh?" Stella drew closer to me, speaking as if she has to keep it a secret from the rest of the world. The mystery ship is sitting right in the middle of the track! Maybe she's right—maybe these seats are the best ones. *How in the world did the ship get there?* She plops right down and makes herself at home as if she could blend right in with the crowd. Stella never talks about the meteor strikes. I think she's mad about it because it's beyond her control.

I sit down feeling like I am taking someone else's seat. Unsure that we will be able to stay in the front row, I hold my purse close in my lap and do not feel settled. "Maybe someone else is sitting here, and we're taking their seats."

"We're not givin' up these seats." Stella means it, speaking in a confident way with her confident reasoning. She speaks softly so that no one can hear but me. "There's nowhere else ta go. So don't even think about it. If someone tries to kick us out, don't even budge. They's gotta be the ones ta go find anotha seat. Not us." Her eyebrows shot up when she put an emphasis on the word *they's*. She looked dead serious when she said *not us*.

Stella is the daughter of an Italian doctor who specializes in sports medicine. She is a people-person who sells Tupperware and hosts monthly parties at other people's houses. She loves being the center of attention. She always wants to be right, and I am discovering that she has savvy business skills, which includes, of course, getting free stuff.

Stella and I are different. She is excited to see all the trucks, but I only have an interest in making it home safe. She stands out like a New York Met on the Brave's baseball field in Atlanta, Georgia, while I blend right in with the crowd. She had moved with her family from the Big Apple to live in a charming southern 'burb near Charlotte, North Carolina.

The mystery ship makes me curious and since the park is well landscaped, I feel somewhat comfortable to be waiting for *round one* to start any minute. Still, I feel like a square peg in a round hole. I can't help but sit here and think about my purpose in life. I decide right now that I am not going to sell Tupperware. *Who am I? I can't just be the lady-who-is-sitting-with-the-Tupperware-lady. What is the meaning of life anyway? Why is half of the world gone?*

* * *

I hear a drum roll over a loudspeaker and then upbeat, energetic music begins. Someone in the crowd whistles when two metal doors swing open and the trucks begin to enter at low speed, an introduction that begs the audience for a big round of applause. The first truck drives right by our section and the audience begins to clap. The lead racer is in a red Chevy Silverado, propped up higher than usual, showing off big tires and shiny wheels. The next racer is in a Ford truck, camouflaged by a green, black, and khaki paint job, dressed in big tires and black wheels. With a limit of thirty trucks in the first round, they drive by one at a time. The third racer waves out the window of a dark gray truck with silver lightning painted down the side. The trucks follow one another to a waiting location where they park on the opposite side of the track. I watch them line up. Piper is the tenth truck and Vinny is the eleventh truck. Just as if they were at an old drive-in movie-theater, thirty trucks park in a long row. I begin to wonder if any of the drivers ever get hurt. How dangerous could it get?

The spectators hear a man's voice on a loud speaker. "We'd like to welcome you to Mr. J's tenth mud racing event. Please remain behind the fence at all times. We hope that you will become a member of the Mud Racing Jamboree while you are here, and you can do so when you stop by the Mud Market, which is where you will also be able to find a souvenir. The Mud Market is located directly behind this track and on your way to *round two*. And in just a moment, we will hear the call to begin. Let's hear it from Mr. J's best fans in the world!"

The crowd cheers wildly.

FINAL SHIPS IN THE NEIGHBORHOOD

I see a young boy sitting next to me, and I ask him a question. "Have you been here before?"

"This is my fifth year! Have you been here before?" He smiles, looking delighted to be sitting in the front row, fully engaged with the race and so are his buddies. The boys must be about ten or eleven years old. It would be awful if the meteor strike hit this location again because now it has over 200,000 people, a big number for a dwindling population.

I have to speak loud to him over the music. "This is my first time."

"You must be real serious to sit in the front row." The boy smiles again and laughs. "The racers try to stay under one minute." He points to a digital clock.

A female voice interjects on the loud intercom. "Once the race begins, we won't stop! Drivers, are you ready?"

A male's voice is heard next. "On your mark, get set, let the race begin!" I hear a gunshot. The shiny red Chevy peels out from the starting line on the back left side of the track, traveling clockwise. The trucks race one at a time against the clock.

The boy next to me whispers something to his buddies. They point at me and laugh.

"What's so funny?" I suddenly feel as if they know something that I don't know.

He says something, but I can't hear. It sounds like he might have said the number *five*.

I want to know what he said. "What?"

He points to the digital clock. He seems enthusiastic about the surroundings, thrilled to have a good view, and on the edge of his seat, squirming back and forth, as did the rest of his buddies.

I look at the digital clock and see the numbers turning. The red truck speeds up a ramp, flies in the air, and lands in the mud. Then it travels in a clockwise direction at full speed and turns, sort of sideways, when going around the bend.

The boy yells again to his buddies. "Eighteen!"

Eighteen? Why is this boy saying eighteen? Here comes the red truck. It's going to pass by. It is so loud! Oh no, it's coming close to the fence right in front of us! Is it going to hit the fence?

"Twenty-five!" the boy yells.

As the truck makes a sliding right-hand turn and passes by our section, it surprisingly flings a huge amount of mud up into the air, most of which land in the first few rows. There is no time to move out of the way. I can hardly believe what is happening. Mud is flying directly at us! We get hit. *I had no idea!* Stella and I have blotches of mud on us—a glob of mud on my shirt, another glob of mud on my pants. Mud on one foot and one flip-flop. Mud on one side of my purse.

"Are you kiddin' me?" Stella looks shocked. She happened to get more mud on her than I did. "I need to get me one of them pieces of cardboard on a stick."

I see the boy next to me and his buddies are scrunched down on the floor, hunching in a ball as low as they could get. The boys pop up and point at me, laughing hysterically. They jump up and down with great excitement. I'm speechless, sitting in a new outfit, decorated in mud.

"Get ready for the next one," the boy yells out.

I look at Stella, and she looks at me.

"I had no idea. Did you?" I see that she is caught off guard just like I had been.

She hardly shakes her head no, and all we can do is break out into a laugh.

FINAL SHIPS IN THE NEIGHBORHOOD

The next gunshot goes off too soon, and I see the camouflaged Ford truck going up the ramp. I look behind me and see spectators with a piece of cardboard that reads ROUND ONE: THIRTY TRUCKS.

Thirty trucks! Why didn't I notice the sign before?

There is no time to hide. The camouflaged Ford takes a big sideways spin when it makes a long right-hand turn, flinging even more mud up into the air this time. I am a little more prepared this time, covering my face while hoping the truck doesn't slam into the fence. A big glob of mud lands in my hair. It is the second layer of mud that lands on us.

Stella calls out to a worker in the stand. "Hey! Excuse me! We need two of those signs!"

The worker happens to know what Stella wants even though the worker is far away.

"You gotta duck when the truck comes around." The boy's words of wisdom speak a little too late.

"Oh, I see. You duck when the clock says twenty-five. Right. I get it now." I notice the next truck ready to peel out.

The third gunshot went off.

Here we go again. This is going too fast!

"Haven't you ever been to Sea World?" the boy asks me. "I went to Sea World before it was destroyed. I sat in the front row and got drenched!"

There is no time to think about his question because I am looking for cardboard. Stella is desperately waiting for the worker to make her way over to us. The dark gray truck takes a lop-sided landing off the ramp. It lands on the back right tire and then on the front right tire.

"Do you always sit in the front row?" I ask the boy to my left.

"It's the only way to go!" He smiles.

109

Stella becomes impatient, stands up, and reaches out her arm. "Hurry up! I NEED TWO OF THOSE!"

"Hey, excuse me, miss! You better sit down!" a person yells from behind.

The worker stumbles over to Stella the best she can and places two cardboard signs in Stella's hands.

Stella hands me a sign, and we see the clock turn twenty-five. *Oh no! The third truck is getting too close to us! Is it going to hit the fence?* I hold the cardboard up in front of my face. I hear a sliding squelch. *Splat!* A loud motor roars a fine tune and speeds to the finish line. This time, a glob of mud sticks onto the back of my shirt.

So it goes, on and on, where trucks are zooming off the ramp, sliding into a right-hand corner U-turn at full speed ahead, and sliding way too close to our section while mud flies up in the air. I see Piper and Vinny and all the rest of the trucks race right by us. Finally, fifteen winners from round one are announced. The crowd walks away perplexed when the announcer makes a final announcement. He reveals how the mystery ship had arrived during the third strike.

"A quantum leap?" I try hard to imagine a ship teleporting. It can't be possible. There has to be another explanation.

"Who would'a eva thought that Vinny and Pipa would make it to round two?" Stella is proud of her man.

I suddenly want to explore the ship. "Did you hear what that guy just said?"

"Neva gunna get me ta know about physics," Stella says. "But if that's what they say, then that's what they say."

No wonder why so many people flocked to this mud race. They really want to see the ship. Maybe some of the news reports were correct. Maybe some of the strange things that have been happening do relate to a *quantum leap*. Other reports say it is some type of annihilation. "Do people really think that the ship was in the ocean one minute, and the next minute it's in a mudflat?"

"I know. Right? Don't believe everything you hear." Sometimes Stella sounded like a tape recorder, spitting back information that someone else had told her, but acting as if she's speaking for herself.

"How do you think it got there?"

"Beats me. I'm not goin' anywhere near that thing. Ya might end up in the Bermuda Triangle. Maybe we oughta walk around with a life jacket, just in case." Stella laughs at her joke.

"So no one can go in the mystery ship?"

"Nope. Must be haunted. Gotta be. It gives me the creeps. Look at it. But the otha' ship, the one ova by the next race, now that one's gunna be impressive."

"How so?"

"Don't cha watch the news? NASA made it. It can hold like 10,000 people. You can stay the night in it."

"Oh, yeah. That does sound familiar. What's it called? It's the cruise-ship-sitting-on-dry-ground. I did hear about it."

"It's called the Galaxy Oasis. And you know what they say?"

"What?"

"At any second, it's going to end up in the ocean. That's why it's sold out. People want to go for a ride in it."

"But it's going nowhere." I can't wrap my head around this information. I look at my watch. We have time to see it before Piper races again. I hope I make it out of this place alive because my book is waiting for me in Piper's truck.

An Afterword to this story is on page 206.

11

THE RISE AND FALL OF KING DABBOLT

by
Laura Stafford

Rena fumbled with the crystal, tossing it in the leather satchel. It was just for show anyway, just a pretty rock—not a tool—and she doubted her ability to see visions at all, until today.

Instinctively, she wanted to tell Afred, but it would be weeks before he returned to continue her tutelage, and if the vision was truth, he may never return at all. Thus, the vision required Rena to act, rather than thoughtfully consider - something she was not yet accustomed to doing, as a simple apprentice. Her standing was higher than that of a servant, but not by much.

Darting back and forth about the room, looking for her boots, her cloak, and her mittens, Rena hopped about, unsure of what to do next, where to go, indecisive, her brain running down every possible and impossible path of every choice she was faced with in this dilemma.

The vision insisted she go to the king, or at least someone

of higher rank and divulge the message. However, in doing that, she would miss her standing appointment with the queen in her chambers. Where she would do the standard fortune telling routine? What suitor would come to her bedside that week and those sorts of things? Rena would certainly be punished for not arriving at the time assigned.

But if she stayed her appointment and neglected to go directly to the king, Rena would be punished for withholding imperative information that directly relates to welfare of the kingdom and its people.

Rena was sweating. Was that treason? Would they hang her? Was it withholding information if you only withheld it for a while? How long did she have before the vision came to be?

That question led her down another meandering path of what-ifs. What if the vision had already occurred? What if the vision was symbolic? Then what did it mean? How should she explain it to the king's men? Would they even listen without Afred's presence?

Moving on instinct like an animal, Rena ran down the steps to the main chambers below where Afred kept residence, and alit down the longer flight that led to the courtyard.

The court bustled, moving like an unchoreographed dance that swayed to the beat of the tolling blacksmith, pounding and threshing, children calling mingled with the singsong laughter of the maidens in the square, the shuffling stomp and soft neighing of the horses. All of this Rena ignored, striding across the muddy yard through puddles of stagnant rain to see the magistrate.

His quarters were tiny and dishevelled, matching the man's demeanor. Harg was a cruel soul, punishing and tactless, and Rena did not like him, but he was the one person who would have the right advice in the absence of the wizard.

He admitted her cautiously and Rena reiterated the vision. He nodded several times without commenting, until she finished by explaining the dilemma she found herself in.

"You've done the right thing," Harg said. "I will escort you, and you will tell the king just as you have told me."

Rena never liked appearing before the king. When she was younger, and she still played with the other little girls in the village, they would pine for Prince Dabbolt - who was much older, daft, and handsome for a boy of his age and stature. They would prance in front of him, hoping to catch his fancy as the next queen who would be lavished by this powerful boy and his family riches. But when he reached marrying age, Dabbolt chose the overbearing, doughy daughter of Duke Rurta. She had smiled shamelessly the day Dabbolt's father had passed on and Dabbolt was crowned.

Unfortunately, Rurta's influence quickly infiltrated the weak-willed brain of not-so-bright Dabbolt, and the kingdom faced the devastating hardship of Rurta's greed - children and the elderly dying in their sleep, freezing, starving.

Rena recognized how lucky she was to have her teacher to care for her. The other girls as old as she, had men to care for them and their livelihood, as well as their children. She knew that at 17-years-old, she should have been married and with child already, but those earthly pleasures left her wanting when the elementals communed with her. There were, of course, many jokes amongst those same little girls, who had grown up to wed these beastly men, that Rena's lover was Afred—a joke in and of itself because of Afred's significantly advanced age—his decision in choosing Rena to understand the powers of nature and magic were solely based on his desire to see his knowledge passed down to someone who would, could and did, understand.

FINAL SHIPS IN THE NEIGHBORHOOD

Rena would not die in the street as many were wont to do, but neither could she approve of the king's strategies. Rurta's influence shadowed even that of Afred. Rena had a feeling that this vision was a response to the current political endeavors. Unlike most women, Rena had special privilege to the political information of the kingdom, because Afred told her everything.

"It will be your place," he had told her confidentially, "to know and see all! Even if they exclude you because you are a woman, you need to hone your skills and powers of observation, train your ear and learn your habits to know what the agenda is and which agenda it is you're playing to."

Rena had nodded in complete understanding. Afred had been the previous king's trusted advisor. Afred had a good heart and his decisions were made with the village's best intentions in mind, as opposed to Rurta. Dabbolt's father had been a fair man but Dabbolt was a blundering fool. Those minor changes in leadership had changed the small kingdom into a squalid hovel of decay and disease.

The new plan was to take wealth from others. Rena called it stealing, but Rurta and Dabbolt called it conquering. They prepared the ships for *conquering* and now the battalions of sailors sailed from port, destined to arrive by surprise on the shores of Forn where the soldiers would gather food, goods, and anything of value.

Whether stealing or conquering, the vision had shown Rena something unimaginable, something no one was expecting, and Rena couldn't honestly say whether it was real or metaphorical.

Harg practically pushed her down the dank hallway that led to the king's chambers, and after a momentary word with the sentries at the door, they were admitted to the receiving room. It smelled of dogs, rotten meat, sour grapes, and vomit.

King Dabbolt sat back in an ornamented chair that sagged under his bulging belly. His fat fingers fed his gnashing mouth an endless supply of dried pheasant, cheese, and bread that crumbled onto his mouldy beard and chest. He made slapping, slurping, grunting noises that echoed about the warm stone room.

Harg jabbed Rena in the back of the leg, driving her to a kneeling position. "Your Highness," she greeted, bowing her head and waiting permission to speak.

"What have you to say, scallion?" Rena didn't know if the king was referring to her or Harg, so she kept silent till the magistrate slapped her ear.

"A vision, your majesty," she answered quickly. "I have seen the tragedy at Fron and beg of you to message the ships to return. Fear and death will hold this kingdom if we continue our path."

"Ridiculous girl. Why do you waste my time with political trivialities?" King Dabbolt laughed, spraying bits of food and spittle. "Do you believe I will simply turn our ships around because of the silly dreams of some girl? What do you know of a king's strategies for leading a kingdom to prosperity?"

Rena was caught off-guard. "A dream?" she recoiled. "It was a *vision*. In water. The people of Fron will retaliate. They will fight back. Our ships will be swallowed by their powerful magic. Our men and boys will die, and we will have gained nothing."

"Show me," the king said, gesturing a greasy hand toward the crystal pouch that hung about her waist.

"Show you? The vision? In the crystal?"

"Yes," he instructed.

"Surely your majesty understands that I cannot recreate a

vision. The Fates show us what they want, when they want, and allow us to make the decisions based on the knowledge we have been given. I cannot show you anything in the crystal, but I can tell you that the very seas will open up and eat our ships."

Rena was escorted gruffly from the chambers, leaving Harg to defend his decision to bring a mindless nag in front of the court.

* * *

Little did King Dabbolt and his petulant advisor know, the magic of Fron was very powerful, derived from the fiery volcanoes that had created the islands. Fron's sorcerer was a wise man who understood its forces, its uses, and how to use that energy for good, for the well-being of his people, whom he loved and desired to see prosper as well.

But as with every good reign, the people knew there would be strife. They saved food from the fertile land, collected rainwater, and cared for their meager supplies with reason and delicacy.

It was Jerob the Wizard who called the people together, the king of Fron standing to his right and a step behind.

"We must stand fast!" Jerob cried out. "Our will must be a collective voice! We can be saved! We are strong! Will you help your king retain his throne?"

Their exulting shouts echoed over the land, the volcano, the flora and fauna, and out to the great seas beyond.

* * *

Rena, freed of her burden, felt defeated and angry rather

than the relief she had expected. She stormed back to her chambers and paced, her mind a whirling dervish, a cacophony of contradictory thoughts she could not control.

The king would do nothing. Afred, and all the most powerful men in the kingdom would be lost, leaving the rest of them defenseless. If the king thought her a fool, what chance did she have of saving anyone?

The washbasin sat on the table, now translucent and calm. Rena went to it and gazed at its halcyon surface, willing it to again reveal its secrets. She focused, concentrating and she felt her mind bending and twisting, blurring her eyesight till colors began swirling in front of her eyes.

With a snapping noise, the vision instantly dissipated, and a tumultuous clattering arose up the stairs to echo in her rooms. The heavy door slammed open to a tumbling awkward group of three men in soldier's garb. Rena had never seen them before and knew they must be the boys recruited to maintain law while the men were off conquering.

"What do you want?" she spat at them.

"By order of Her Majesty The Queen, you are required to present yourself for due punishment regarding your offenses." It was a memorized speech to be repeated without incident. Rena was sure this boy was not able to read from an official arresting scroll.

Although Rena already knew why they were here, she argued anyway. "I have done nothing wrong," she said with conviction.

He sighed, hunching his shoulders. "Miss, I don't know your offense, but I'd be much obliged if you just came with us without an argument."

Rena sighed too. She didn't want to go without a fight, but this boy was so obviously defeated already. She followed him to the queen's sitting room where she was holding "court".

"Your Highness," Rena saluted, bowing deeply.

"You, Rena of the Galens, are charged with Failing To Report At An Assigned Point In Time. How say you?" the queen lifted her peaked nose high and sniffed below half-closed eyes.

Rena showed only the barest amount of respect. "I had royal business that demanded the attention of the king. Surely you'd have me attend to official business before responding to a weekly reading of your fortunes. The king can vouch for my presence. And so can Harg!"

The queen snorted. "I care nothing for your excuses girl. You will spend a week in the dungeon." She huffed. "And I'm supposing your precious wizard can't save you, seeing as how he's out to sea. Take her away. Bread and water only."

Rena did not struggle. Something in her gut told her it would be in her best interest to take the punishment without a fight. She allowed the boys to lead her away.

* * *

In every bowl of water she was brought, Rena saw the vision. It was the same every time. People chant from the shores, the ground begins to shake and the mountains begin to smoke like a lightning strike in a dead forest. The shaking gets stronger and the people sway with the motion, rocking in rhythm to the thunder that comes from the earth. And then the very water of the seas begins to swirl and open, the water in the bowl spins like a whirlpool, and the vision of her own people's ships sinks to the bottom of the bowl, swallowed and eaten.

And when the vision is faded, Rena is so exhausted, so

thirsty and so hungry, that she wastes no time gulping the water from the worm-eaten wood and crunching the stale bread between dry lips.

She counted the days by the number of moons and on the sixth day, a tumult arose outside. Screams and shouts filled the air, Rena could smell smoke and fire, she could hear tearful calls and the cracking of whips, men begging for mercy.

But she could see nothing. No one came to the dungeon. She was without water to gaze, without protection and without knowledge.

On the seventh day, the world quieted outside and she could hear nothing except the distinct crackling of fire and the wind whispering through the gaps in the granite.

She waited.

No one came—no guards, no servant boys, no kitchen dregs with bread and water. She cried herself to sleep, knowing she would waste away to nothing in the moldy, smelly pits of the castle, like so many others before her.

* * *

The sound of bells woke Rena from a dreamless sleep. There was a tall, handsome young man in robes standing at the thick iron bars.

"Is this her?" he asked.

Afred stepped out from the shadows behind the regal man. "Yes, she is the one. Hello, Rena."

"Afred!" she gasped. "I thought you were dead!"

The other man waved his hand at the bars and the gate opened with an audible click and creak.

"Rena, this is the wizard Jerob," Afred said reverently.

"Jerob? But...I don't understand..."

"We knew of Rurta's plan. We knew of Dabbolt's weakness," Afred explained as they climbed out of the dungeons. "We have been collaborating."

The two wise men nodded to each other. "Now we are rulers of this kingdom. And you are our royal sorceress," Jerob laughed with a gleam in his eye.

"But, Rurta? Dabbolt?" Rena shook her head, the confusion waning and realization dawning.

"Dead," Afred sighed.

"My vision...?"

"Real," Jerob countered.

"We will not tolerate evil. We serve the good of our people, not the good of ourselves. Do you agree?" Jerob and Afred gazed at her intently.

"Yes!" Rena shouted with bold conviction.

"Then you are with us?" Jerob questioned.

Again, Rena reverberated, "Yes!"

Rena pulled the crystal from her pouch and handed it to Afred. "You're sure?"

"It's just a rock," she replied. "Let's go eat."

An Afterword to this story is on page 207.

12

THE LAST DAWN II

by
Christian Warren Freed

Fifteen years had passed since we discovered that the world was not destroyed. Fifteen years, when hope and the promise of rebuilding had been lost, gripped Harbor in unprecedented prosperity. We were officially sworn into the new United States, a welcome for us, which we would soon learn was a growing community.

Much of the technology from before was lost; some of it was lost forever. The days of computers and Internet were long gone. I vaguely remembered going to watch a movie once, but such things were best left forgotten. Perhaps one day the world will advance back to where it had been. Perhaps not. I knew I'd never see those days renewed. Time was as much my enemy now as destiny.

"Major, we're ready to embark."

I turned to the young seaman and nodded. "Give the word. Set sail at once."

He saluted and ran off barking orders to the engine crews. Soon massive columns of steam pumped from our fires. My uniform felt good, like it belonged. Our lives changed for the better the day the cavalry column rode into Harbor, and we learned the world hadn't ended. Many of us joined the reconstituted army. I relished the thought of traveling the world, seeing sights that most others would never get the opportunity to. My desires took me into the fledgling navy and brought me to the bridge of my own steam cruiser, the *Resilience*. My task was simple: patrol the Snake River and keep bandit attacks to a minimum. For five years I rode the waters, fighting when necessary and protecting constantly.

The navy consisted of two score steam cruisers built mostly from timber. Back up, sails were stored in the holds, reminding me of the stories I once read as a child: *Moby Dick* and *Mutiny on the Bounty*. Without power, most of the once formidable ships of the world either sank or rusted away, leaving broken skeletons as grim reminders of what once was. But that was the past. Now was the time to look forward, to re-imagine what could be.

Towns and villages sprung up, expanding the new American empire. My heart lightened upon seeing so much life. Trees, bushes, and wild flowers covered the land. Birds and animals returned. I felt as if nothing more could go wrong and the worst was over. We'd survived. Our world endured and humanity was given a second chance to prove itself before the eyes of God. That's when I received a message to return to New Richland immediately.

My heart hammered without knowing why. Foul portents clouded my horizon. We'd heard rumors of a strange explosion just south of the city. Quakes and tremors ripped new tears in the land. Dozens died instantly in a flash of light. Hundreds more were injured. Most of the truth was speculation. People whispered of every possible scenario from a nuclear bomb to asteroids. *How much more can we take before we just throw up our hands and give in?*

The trip upriver to New Richland went quickly, and I soon found myself reporting to WestCom headquarters. Guards saluted and rushed me in. I was clearly expected. *Why me? I'm not important, just one man in the middle of this.* My nerves started acting up when a young lieutenant escorted me into the commanding officer's waiting room.

"Ah, Major Haversham, come in," Admiral Pelty said upon seeing me.

"Yes sir," I replied and took a nervous seat in front of his desk.

Banners and old awards filled the walls; all accolades of a man who'd done something. I couldn't help but feel a little jealous.

He rubbed his bald head. "Steven, I'm going to level with you. I don't like it when my officers have personal affairs that interfere with the navy. We don't need it. Bad for morale and a waste of time doing the paperwork."

A lump formed in my throat as I raced through everything I'd said or done since joining the service.

"Sir, might I ask what is this all about? I'm scheduled to go on maternity leave in two days. Molly is having our third child." I stammered.

He fixed me with his steel gaze. "Your cousin William has been sighted at last."

William! The man had become the bane of my existence. Ever since the elders and I had him banished from the harbor, he'd been trouble. William linked up with a band of mutants and pillaged his way up and down the rivers. How many bodies were left in their wake was never known, but he'd quickly become the most wanted man west of the Mississippi

River. Hunting him down was one of the navy's top priorities, and it seemed I had been given the unenviable task. Just like that all thoughts of leave vanished.

"What are my orders?" I asked. There wasn't any point in beating around the bush.

"Capture if practical. Terminate if not, but there is more." He paused and I felt my stomach try to rip free. "I'm sure you've heard of the explosion. As best we can figure a small asteroid struck just between what used to be Walla Walla and Kennewick. Casualties weren't as bad as you might expect, but my recon teams have brought back certain classified information."

I hesitantly accepted the black and white photos being shoved at me. Worse, I struggled to make sense of it.

"Yes, Major. It's a ship, but not one of ours. If I were a superstitious man, I'd say it was alien in nature," he said.

Alien? You've got to be kidding me. Aliens don't exist. "Sir, I don't understand what this has to do with William."

"Your cousin and his merry band were last seen boarding this same ship and setting off south."

I wanted to groan. Not only had William resurfaced, but he'd appropriated a potentially alien ship for his crimes. "If he makes it to the ocean…" I let the thought die. We both knew if William made it to the ocean, he'd be free to take his evil across the world. He had to be stopped.

"Find him, Steven. Stop him before it's too late."

* * *

The *Resilience* powered south at full steam. Time was running out. We'd passed several burned out villages along the way. Smoke still pumped from a few. Crows and vultures circled over the dead, confirming my fears that William had gone insane. Perhaps it was from his exposure to the mutants. Perhaps just from being exiled so many years ago. Regardless, he needed to be stopped. Once I managed to get past the sheer carnage, I started looking more closely, trying to discern any patterns in William's behavior that might give him away. I needed to find a weakness, fast.

My engineers and I poured over reports and the photos of the mysterious ship. We were each baffled. The sleek lines of the hull reminded me of an old battleship, pointed at the bow to slice through the water quicker. But any similarities ended there. A strange, round turret sat aft. We could only assume from the snub nose barrel protruding from the end that it was the primary weapon system. We also noticed the ship didn't so much go into the water but skimmed the surface. There wasn't anything human made on Earth with such capabilities. *We might be in serious trouble.*

I excused myself and went to the quarterdeck. A sliver of moon cast pale reflections down from a cloudless sky. Mount Hood dominated the sky to our left. I'd never seen it before and wished I had more time to enjoy the majesty, but the hunt was on. William was close. This was my most favorite time of day. All of the troubles of the day fled under the cover of night. My only regret was that Molly and I were not together. She'd been a good sort, strong enough to stick by me when I needed and even when I didn't. Getting married was the right thing to do. Now I questioned if I'd ever see her again.

The alien ship scared me. I didn't like going up against something I didn't know. Bravery was never my strong suit. I was better as a librarian, but the harshness of our times demanded me to step up. Suddenly, I spied something in the water: wreckage of some sort. Bits of flotsam drifted past.

Char blackened pieces of wood and half slagged metal. The first body had gone by, before my mind processed what I was seeing, and then another body and another. William must have sunk a merchant ship.

I grabbed the nearest handset and ordered, "All hands general quarters! Battle stations!"

The *Resilience* came alive with the bustle of seventy men rushing to take their positions. Cannons were loaded. Rifles armed and boarding parties staged. I grabbed my flak vest and donned my rather worn helmet upon entering the bridge. "Report."

"Sir, we've confirmed this was the merchant vessel *Oberon*. Forward lookouts report seeing our prey three hundred meters ahead. Orders, sir?"

He was hesitant in naming our enemy alien. We all were. That changed nothing. "Charge the forward guns and bring us into range. I want that ship at the bottom of the river."

The *Resilience* steamed ahead, or maybe the alien ship slowed. Darkness made it difficult to tell. I did know they fired first. A massive ball of blue-green energy came spitting from their rear gun. The hairs on my arms stood on end. My skin prickled. Suddenly, it grew extremely hot. My eyes flew wide. "Brace for impact!"

We narrowly missed the full force of the blast thanks to the quick thinking of our helmsman. I made a mental note to recommend him for commendation when we returned to port—if we returned. "First officer, are we in range?"

"Aye, Sir."

Anger flashed. "Fire!"

Three 105mm cannons belched round shot. Flames trailed after. Watching through binoculars, I saw the rounds bounce harmlessly from the strange metal shell. Power collected around their weapon. They were getting ready to fire again. We only had one chance of surviving. "Helm, get us as close as possible. They won't be able to risk firing without destroying themselves in the process."

I avoided the bridge crew's looks. I didn't need them to know I was crazy. That was the easy part to figure out. I lifted my binoculars and kept trying to find any exploitable weakness. My heart thundered as I spied William stepping onto the back deck. His smile told me everything. "Deck gunners, take that man out now!"

Rifle fire spit from the gun emplacements on the upper deck. Most of it ricocheted with barely a spark. One struck William in the shoulder. A tiny plume of blood fountained and he pitched back. They fired. Men screamed briefly. Superheated waves crashed against our hull, nearly tipping us. The alien ship sped away, sharply turning right and ducking behind a small island in the middle of the river.

"Don't lose him!" I shouted unnecessarily. Three of my bridge crew were down. Many of the others were dazed. Thankfully the helmsman was still thinking and we powered up the river. Fires burned across the waters. I couldn't help but feel like we had already lost. Balling my hand into a fist, I slammed it into the polished wood railing to my right. *Catch him. Catch him.*

We emerged from the island and my worst fears were confirmed. The alien ship was already hundreds of meters away and pulling further. They were so far away that William didn't bother firing back on us. I wanted to scream and bellow my frustrations to the heavens. Not that it mattered. William had won. His escape was certain, and I knew he'd return one day to make us all pay for my ineptitude. *What have I done?*

I watched the alien ship slip past the fangs of land, closing in on the bay and into the night no less. I had failed. William, while wounded, had escaped with his band of mutants and an alien technology we couldn't match. The ship disappeared under a pale halo. Reprimand coming, I ordered the *Resilience* about and began the long trip back to New Richland.

Only now did I let my thoughts drift back to Molly. Another day lost. Another important moment in *our* life I wasn't there for. I knew she'd forgive me, but that didn't make the anticipation of our next meeting any easier. The *Resilience* steamed on into the night. It was time to go home.

An Afterword to this story is on page 208.

13

THE MYSTERY OF THE SINKING SHIPS

by
Shae Hamrick

Amber glanced across the ship's railing at the waves. So much had changed in just a few years. Here she was, traveling the ocean in search of...what exactly? Some mysterious force that was sinking ships and killing people?

Amber turned to watch her brother, John. He paced the deck, his head down and his hands behind his back. He hadn't wanted want to come, but she needed someone who she could trust. After the devastation, many had turned to robbing and killing just to survive. Who better to protect her than her brother? He had escaped with her when the asteroid crashed into the mountains, not far from their home, in the northern US. The impact shifted the faults and created volcanic eruptions that destroyed nearly everything around them.

She shivered. Best to leave it in the past and move on. Her training at the science institute afterward had been intense, and she wanted nothing more than to relax for a bit. Her professor, Dr. Fredrick, had invited her to join him on this expedition—all bills paid. He needed a research assistant in order to get the grant and she fit the bill. Her job? Keep track of his notebooks. Who could ask for better? Well, except that keeping track of them had proved more difficult than she expected. He was in the habit of laying them down as he discussed some bit of trivia and would forget where he left them. So, like a puppy, she tagged along wherever he went and picked them up after him.

Speaking of ... where had he gone?

Amber searched the deck. A lone notebook flapped in the wind near an open porthole. She sighed and walked over to pick it up. As she reached for it, Dr. Fredrick popped back through the ship's opening.

He smiled. "Always on top of things. Thank you. I was just wondering where I set it." He nodded toward the door. "Come. See what I found."

Amber handed him the notebook as she entered the passageway. The dimness of the interior caused her to stumble. The professor stopped and pointed toward the stairs to the left. She smiled, though she doubted he could see it, and moved carefully that direction. They went down three levels before reaching the lowest level of the cargo holds. As her eyes adjusted, she saw a large hold full of stacked boxes lashed in place with ropes and cargo netting. On the far side were several closed porthole hatches, presumably leading into smaller holds as had been in all the other ships they had traveled.

Dr. Fredrick had spent the last five months checking each shipping route and all the cargo ships he could find, speaking to the crews, and following a trail of death and mystery. Amber was not thrilled about his research subject. Yet, she doubted he would find anything but seamen's superstition in the aftermath of all the turmoil from the asteroid's impact.

She glanced around and realized John hadn't followed. He didn't like the holds or documenting the cargo.

At the professor's indication, Amber walked toward the middle door where a seaman in ragged clothes waited. Dr. Fredrick was searching his pockets. Amber handed him a fresh pencil. He couldn't seem to keep up with them either. She had switched to pencils after he lost the first twenty nice pens she had bought for him. Fortunately, it wasn't her money, but she saw no sense in wasting it either. Resources were scarce now.

The room they entered was dark. Amber stopped. She nearly fell when the professor bumped into her.

"Oh. So sorry. The light is over here." He moved away.

In the near darkness, she could hear the waves lapping against the hold. The smell of dirt, metal, and rusty oil permeated the room. With a click, the room brightened and shrunk. The walls were closer than she expected. In fact, they seemed to bow in the middle to where a large, pitted rock sat. It was three feet in diameter, looking as if it had been beaten with a ball-peen hammer and was covered in seaweed. Amber shook her head.

"Astounding, isn't it?" the professor's voice boomed beside her.

"This?" Her voice came out as a squeak.

As she shifted nearer, his hand stopped her. "I wouldn't get any closer. I haven't discovered where they got this specimen yet, but this is what we have been searching for."

Staring at him, he smiled a goofy grin at her. Her mouth hung open.

Clenching her jaw, she turned to study the ugly hunk of stone and metal. "You have been looking for a rock?"

He nodded and scratched notes on the paper. "Yes, dear.

FINAL SHIPS IN THE NEIGHBORHOOD

And this is not just a rock. This, if I am correct, is part of the asteroid that broke up in the atmosphere. Right here in front of us. There hasn't been such a find since the tragedy."

The room began to sway, and Amber reached out a hand. Something to hold on to...anything. Another piece? How could that be and what was it doing in this ship?

"Easy, dear," the professor said and grabbed her arm. "Are you all right?"

Black spots popped up in front of her eyes and she stepped back. "I...I ..." She wasn't certain. How could that be here? "What did you mean by broke up?"

"Oh, I didn't tell you, did I? Well, the asteroid that they had been positioning past the moon had an ice core with chunks of metal fragments packed on top. Or so they thought. When it broke in space, as they tried to park it, the first part came down in the mountains." He was staring at her with the look her grandfather gave her as a child when he was explaining why her grandmother wouldn't be coming back from the hospital. "A second part came down later and was believed to have fallen into the sea, creating the tsunamis that coursed the African ocean and sunk so many ships."

Amber sat on the floor, the cold metal cooling the heat building in her hands.

"Rumors that it was still sinking ships persisted. The One World Government decided to investigate and offered me the job, only because I was on the team that predicted the pull of the moon and earth's gravity would break apart the asteroid."

The world was fading at the edges as she glowered at him. "You predicted?"

His face drew into the downcast droop of a clown's sad face. "Yes." He knelt down in a crouch. "I am sorry for what you lost. I was hoping that finding this might make up for

133

some of your sorrow. I know you have been studying hard in all of your classes, but I noticed your determination. You have the potential to be on the forefront of preventing the next major asteroid or meteorite catastrophe. I was hoping this might encourage you to work in the space and explorations field."

Standing and turning to the rock, he put his hands on his hips and shook his head. "But first, we have to get rid of this one."

Amber blinked, her vision returning instantly. "What?"

He turned back to her. "Don't you feel it? Can't you see what it's doing to the walls of the ship? Even the waves outside are reacting."

Glancing around, Amber realized that it hadn't been her imagination. The walls were curved inward. So was the ceiling. "That rock is bending the walls?"

Dr. Fredrick nodded. "Yes. It must have a magnetic core. That is why it has been sinking ships and why crews have seemed to go insane. Enough strange happenings, of things moving on their own, and anyone might think they had gone crazy. I just don't know what we are going to do with it out here in the middle of the Atlantic. It took me this whole voyage just to get anyone to admit it was even on the ship."

He pointed to the man standing by the wall and staring wide-eyed at the rock.

A loud bang made them both jump and then it was dark again.

Amber screamed.

"Easy," the professor ordered, grabbing her hand and holding it tight. "The door just closed."

Amber panted. "And the lights?"

"I'm sure they're set to turn off when the door closes to

save on electricity. Remember when we came in?"

Amber hoped so.

"The door is behind you. Let's just make our way back and we can open it again."

Reaching the door first, Amber fumbled with the latch but it wouldn't open. The professor moved her to the side. He then grunted several times.

"Well, it seems stuck."

"No stuck." The voice of the seaman came to them at almost a whisper. "The stone is hungry."

Click, click, click. "The lights won't turn back on. Pedro, don't be silly. The asteroid doesn't eat. It is just a piece of space rock."

Something pushed Amber to the floor and a loud pounding reverberated from the door.

"Let us out! Let us out!"

More pounding.

"Pedro," Dr. Fredrick shouted. "Calm down. Nothing is going to eat us."

Amber scooted along the wall, away from the mad seaman. Her heart pounded faster than Pedro's fists. Her hands found a rope, attached to the wall, and she pulled herself up.

Metal groaned and the floor shifted. Amber clung to the rope as the wall beside her moved. Thudding from the middle of the room, or what used to be the middle, was followed by Pedro's scream and Dr. Fredrick's curse.

Amber's chest tightened. "Professor!"

The lights flickered several times. The room was sideways. The rock rested against the right wall. Both the professor and Pedro had slid across the floor as well. Amber's rope dangled in a winding path across the sideways floor.

As the lights continued flickering oddly, Amber held tight and shifted the end of her rope toward the two men. Pedro frantically grabbed it and scrambled up its length, his movements causing the end to shift erratically. Dr. Franklin managed to grab hold as it passed and followed Pedro. Pedro was getting closer quickly, though, and Amber wasn't certain she wanted him that close. She considered whether to kick him away or just panic.

Before fear ripped her heart out, he stopped at the door and began pounding. Amber closed her eyes. Suddenly, she was sliding toward Pedro. She grabbed the rope tighter. Her arms ached but she didn't want to get closer to either Pedro or that cursed rock.

Staring at the lump of metal and stone, she tilted her head. From this angle, she could see the side. The rock was a mixture of melted nickel-iron and silicates, of almost equal parts, and in an odd dappled pattern. No wonder the walls bent. If it had a solid iron core...

Wham! The door open. Amber almost lost her grip and her heart jumped into her throat.

"Amber," John called.

Pedro was through the door, screaming as he half slid and half clambered away from the port.

"John," Dr. Fredrick managed first. "Are we glad to see you, dear boy. Help Amber out. She can't possibly hold on much longer."

John positioned himself in the port frame and reached for Amber.

She scooted toward him. "How did you find us? What happened? Why is the ship sideways? And how did you get the door unstuck?"

John smiled. Beyond John and along the wall were several

men clinging to a rope net, which spread across the large hold from one corner near the end of the stairs. Their faces reflected the same fear that Pedro had exhibited. Amber wondered if the look on her face was any different.

"Finding you was easy with the ruckus from the pounding."

Dr. Fredrick chuckled. Amber moved through the port and stepped onto the netting while grabbing hold. One of the men clasped her elbow and helped her through as John let go.

"As for the door, we pulled and it opened."

Amber glanced to see it plastered against the wall where the ship leaned.

"The ship," John grunted, and his face reddened as he pulled on Dr. Fredrick's arm, "hit a sandbar on an uncharted volcanic island. The captain wants to see both of you. Seems something is wrong with his instruments. He had just come looking when we hit the sandbar."

Dr. Fredrick grabbed the netting, just below Amber, and moved awkwardly around her toward the stairs. "Good. We may be in luck then. I think I know what caused his trouble and how to solve it. This island may be our salvation."

"Or our death," John said, a grimace drawn across his face.

Amber stopped negotiating the rope netting and stared at him.

John shrugged. "I've never heard of a ship getting free after hitting land."

When they reached the deck, Amber ached all over. She had been jogging daily with John and yoga twice a week, but this climbing around the tilted ship was grueling. She huffed as she rested against one of the beams. The captain and Dr. Fredrick talked in hushed tones.

After a bit, the professor returned to Amber and John.

"Well, we are indeed in luck. The tide is rising and we may be able to shift off this bar. In the meantime, I have convinced the captain that he needs to unload the meteor and leave his prize on this little island for the safety of the crew and his ship. The magnetic field from the asteroid is what caused his instruments to fail and incidentally, the lights to go out in the room.

Amber shifted her weight to face him. "You mentioned it's magnetic."

He smiled as John looked between them both. "Yes. It looks composed of silicate and nickel-iron on the outside. However, the part that is broken off on one side, and is melted, looks to be more of a solid metal. A core chunk of iron would not be out of the question if not rare. That is, after all, what they intended, to mine the asteroid. They just didn't realize what bringing such heavy metals into close proximity of other magnetic bodies with heavy gravitational pulls might do. Sudden acceleration, heating, and poof! It exploded into several pieces and came crashing down like nuclear missiles."

Amber perked up. "Several?"

Dr. Fredrick cocked his head and grimaced. "Yes. But most of them were smaller and had no real impact. Only three were large enough to cause any damage, and two are now accounted for."

"And the third," John asked, his voice cracking.

"Ah. Not to worry, dear boy. It landed somewhere in the ocean. Here in the Atlantic actually. Funny that two of the pieces should end up so close to each other."

Amber's face heated and her hands shook. "What do you mean so close?"

"Well, I can't be certain as the instruments are not

working correctly, but we may well have wandered close to the other fragment. It wouldn't surprise me that it might have caused these small volcanic islands to spring up. We know that the shifting plates did create several new volcanoes all over the world and several inactive ones to become active. It is the reason we need such intelligent young men and women to enter the study of both the asteroids impact and the changing environment."

A loud screech interrupted him, and Amber turned to the hatch over the main hold. She felt the shifting of the ship as the tide rose but now there was a pull toward the middle. Using a boom and winch, the crewmen lowered a cable and net into the hold. Shortly, they lifted it again. The asteroid nestled in the netting. Amber watched with awe as they moved it toward the side. The ship shifted.

Tumbling past John, Amber snatched at everything. She managed to grab a pole. With her heart beating heavy, she clung to the thin metal.

John had landed on the side of one of the beams.

The men around them shouted and clawed at handholds on the ship.

The rock dangled at the end of the hoist, just below her, swinging back and forth wildly. The hoist's control cabin was empty, the operator falling to the other side of the ship.

Refusing to shut her eyes, Amber let go.

She sped toward the winch's control cabin.

With a thump that nearly knocked her breath out, she landed against the door. She opened it carefully. Below her, the other open door gaped. The ship's side looked so very far away. Bracing her feet on the cabin frame, she climbed in.

The rock...the cursed rock...the man-eating, ship-sinking-rock...still swung heavily back and forth. With the water rising, the ship shifted.

As the rock reached its apex, Amber hit the release lever. The rock sailed through the air, landing with a thud on the beach.

Amber scrambled into the seat as the ship righted.

Cheers resounded around the deck.

Later that evening, as the ship drifted out of the treacherous landmasses and the stars rose, Amber leaned against the railing and watched the night slip by.

John came up beside her and nudged her with his shoulder. "That was a brave thing you did."

Amber shook her head. "No. That was just a desperate thing. I hope I never see that rock again."

"So you are giving up?"

Amber punched his arm. "Not on your life. I just don't ever want to see that rock again."

John rubbed his arm and chuckled. "I didn't know you felt so strongly…" He froze, looking past her and to one side.

Amber turned. A cold shiver went up her back and her hands turned to ice as she clutched the rail.

They were passing another small island. On the shore, in the moonlight, sat a rock, glinting and looking much like the one they left behind. Except this one was sticking out of the hull of another ship, lying on its side, on the beach.

"Well, kids," Dr. Franklin's voice startled her from behind. "We're on our way. You wouldn't believe where we ended up. Say good night to the Bermuda Triangle."

An Afterword to this story is on page 209.

14

RESTORATION OF ORDER

by
Amos Parker

Up so high, she seems like a beauty ready to lean, fall, and sink to the ocean bottom.

Captain Matthew Starbuck shook his head, sailing west and knowing enough to dispel the imbalanced image. Fully dressed in Royal Navy power, his bicorn hat kept his short black hair from blowing in the fresh ocean breeze. He looked far down from the crow's nest at the subservient world of brown, white, and crystalline blue.

God in heaven must enjoy heights as well.

Even grounded, the captain stood tall. But up so high, a mighty sensation contrasted with the imbalanced one, helping to dispel it.

He'd taken good schooling. He knew the math of leverage. He knew he carried only a man's weight, not the fearful supernatural weight required for capsizing. But his mind's knowing did not kill his heart's feeling. Not altogether. His fear of the vessel sinking lingered on, like a tumor hidden beneath his rank-decorated chest.

She stands. She will stand. We sail on.

He smiled at the emotion: fear, such childish silliness.

It is better to know than feel.

* * *

The year is 1805 but on an alternate path of reality. Magic coupled with power, both white and black, yet much remained the same.

Known to his crew and throughout the British fleet as Lucky Star, the captain stood in his crow's nest and felt God's hot noonday sun. His eyes burned with sea wind and bright rays. His nostrils flared, breathing Triton's salty mist. Beneath, he felt the solid heft of Her Majesty's *Stormchaser*, a ship of the line, his woman ship of the royal line, sailing hard.

Stormchaser, perhaps, is the world's only worthy and governable one.

Christened as *Stormchaser* not a year before, she all but flew westward with the aid of a potent—collecting a spell—one costing the lives of two royal magicians. None questioned the merit of the price. So *Stormchaser* hurtled onward, in the service of her captain, the crew, and the civilized world's mortal quest. Nothing save the ultimate and, for a craft so large, neigh uncastable spell for true flight could ever outclass her.

The captain chuckled. His fingers stroked the reinforced rim on the crow's nest.

No pride is heavy enough to lever her sidelong into the sea.

Beneath the captain, the fine African oak creaked with sway, wood constituting *Stormchaser's* masterwork hull. She sailed so steady it seemed she could bear a mainmast that reached God himself as well as all the cloud-white sailcloth of heaven.

He looked down. All around below him, her unfurled white sails flapped and snapped, woven of the finest spell-strengthened terrestrial white.

Non-officer crewmen climbed in her rigging like clothed monkeys, seeming like ticks. To Lucky Star, their climbing emphasized the fact that so many of his men harbored simple minds not civilized enough to destroy superstition.

Officers knew better. But non-officers, often uneducated, believed in…the Jonah.

Jonah….

At the name, at the mental echo of the infuriating superstitious notion, the captain's hard, weatherworn fingers squeezed the nest. They did so in emotional, uncivilized betrayal of him, flouting his mind's intellect. The hands, at the behest of the heart, wished for something, something terrible, something unacknowledged on high.

The notion of a Jonah, of a corrupted crewman sewing evil, filled him with fury the way the best sails fill with the foul winds of a dark, energetic storm.

Civilization's mortal crisis fanned the primitive flames of his emotion. An ensuing fury beat on the high rock of his mind like a hurricane sea, blackening it.

Why could he not stamp out the spell of the Jonah?

But it seemed no surviving ship could. The superstition infected every civilized vessel. And yet Lucky Star once convinced himself that *Stormchaser*, Her Majesty's mightiest ship, under the governance of the Royal Navy's mightiest captain, could and would rise above any Jonah as though a crow's nest on God's own mainmast.

Half the ships of the civilized world all vanished but for splinters. France. Spain. Even America. Every inch of the Civilization's Imperial

World.

Lucky Star's fingers squeezed harder on the African wood. It held.

But ships of the Her Majesty's Royal Navy are not infested with corrupt, evil crewmen. Jonahs are fantasy creatures, imagined as a notion of infernal and devil-bound.

He frowned, eyes drinking the visible world, but he saw another real world.

Yet, I can't speak for other navies.

He smiled. France, perhaps, a fancy country of fancies, might have Jonahs.

And then the anger took him again.

"Fantasy! Ticks bleeding reality."

His jaw worked.

It is a real enemy England faces. It is a conspiracy of cannon fire and can be fired upon with cannons. It may be piracy's cancer. Perhaps a coven of rebels: fools battling the white sail's burden. We will sink anything to blame for evil. I will on this voyage, though due home months ago. With the God-saved queen as my witness, we will track down the primitive things and send them bubbling to the depths of hell!'

A white gull flew past.

To the starboard north, a pod of sperm whale breached through the surface of the water and blew, forcefully expelling air through the blowhole. The captain unlocked a hand from the unbreakable African wood and raised it, smiling and saluting their black leviathan bulks.

Spermaceti is not our treasure today, fellow vessels. I absolve you and your terrible jaws.

And with perfect, impervious balance, *Stormchaser* sailed on.

* * *

"Captain!"

Lucky Star footed down the rope ladder and through the rigging. Boots striking deck, he heard his booming commander's cry. Commander Pillion, a man as lean, straight and strong as a spell-crafted iron beam, strode across the deck to his captain. He saluted, face tight. He pointed below deck.

"Three in the crew have turned on Lieutenant Tegene. They have him confined, guarded below deck. They expect you, as if in respect."

The captain faced Commander Pillion sidelong, raising eyebrows.

"This is a joke, Commander. Your poor taste in humor leaks coin, like a torn lady's purse."

"No, Captain."

"Then try a good joke, Commander."

Commander Pillion shook his head. "It was not a joke, Captain."

The Captain, turning full toward Commander Pillion, reddened. He boomed. "What? And irons do not bind them already?" Lucky Star closed his eyes, mastering emotions. "Leaving them unchained is altogether broke humor, Commander."

Eyes darting, the commander's face darkened.

"It is not so easy, Sir."

"I order it to ease then. You need a captain's authority for easement?"

"Sir! Lieutenant Castor is one of them! And the crew supports him. You know the crew idolizes Castor."

Lucky Star looked away from the commander. He saw, all around, eyes of the on-duty crew keeping steady gazes on their conversation. But the weight of the myriad eyes did not buckle the captain. He could not topple the ship from the crow's nest, and superstitious eyes could topple him.

Controlled anger, a due anger at treason, blossomed in the captain. It came out as a fine sculpture of rage.

"Then tell me! What is the meaning of this... treason?"

His voice, a god-like bellow, came near to shaking the very ship. Half of the crew broke stares, turning eyes downward. The captain, noticing the odor of seagoing sailors, turned from Pillion, stomping to the nearest of them. A man, swarthy in a bandana and called Radagast, cringed. With his mighty fingers, the captain seized the far shorter six-foot man by his soiled collar, lifting him to eye level.

His voice hummed with a waiting storm's controlled fury.

"I asked a question, seaman. What is the meaning of this treason? Tell me, or I will pack your head into a cannon and sink a whale for sperm."

Radagast tried to swallow, but the knuckles of the captain pressed into his throat and under his jaw. Coughing, the sailor nodded. Lucky Star released him to speak, and Radagast fell a foot to the deck, stumbling.

"We... we... we...."

Radagast coughed again. The captain put a hand on his fine eight-shot pistol's engraved silver handle.

"Are you a pig, seaman? Are you going to *wee* all the way home?"

Radagast shook his head. The captain felt the large crew's tense silence all around him. He felt wide eyes staring. Pillion cleared his throat but said nothing. At last, hacking, Radagast spoke.

"No...C...Captain."

"Then tell me the reason for the treason!"

Radagast swallowed. "Tegene is the Jonah! He will sink us,

like the others!"

Lucky Star frowned. "Insubordination, seaman. I gave my orders regarding the beliefs of my crew."

"It is the truth! We all know! That African—"

Lucky Jack roared. "Her Majesty chose that *African* herself! He is proof that none need stay uncivilized! Do you defy your queen? Shall I keep you chained in the dark and in irons until I drag you before her so you may tell her yourself?"

Radagast looked down, shaking his head and shaking everywhere, unable to speak.

"Speak, seaman!"

Radagast, with a mighty effort, lifted his head and spoke.

"The devil sent him to avenge our plundering of his Dark Continent and all of his world's heathens! Tegene is a dark wizard!"

The commander interjected. "Captain. If I may—"

Lucky Star whirled on the voice. "You may not!" He whirled back to Radagast. "You."

He leaned in, close to the seaman's ship-bound stink.

"Seaman. There is no more discerning white wizard in the world than the queen's own Koda. He is as cleansed of heathen ways as Tegene, or more so, and just as yearning to hunt for Her Majesty's colonies."

Lucky Star grinned, an idea coming to him. He pushed his face near Radagast's.

"Yet Tegene recalls the dark, heathen ways just as the queen can recall the orders for treason's torture. She fancies the iron maiden, seaman. Aye. Perhaps, in irons, you will tell the queen she has been fooled by her dear Koda, and tell him that he lies?"

Blanching and quaking, Radagast looked down at his feet. "No, C…Captain."

Lucky Star stood back. "Then what will you do, seaman?"

Lucky Star drew his pistol with one hand and lifted the head of Radagast, by the hair, with the other. He pulled back the gun's sculpted hammer, and the noise of the click defeated all audible competition. Then, pressing the end of the barrel hard into the bone between the man's eyes, the captain repeated himself.

"What will you do?"

Radagast stuttered.

"I...I...I..."

"That was not an aye or no question, seaman."

"I will say...all hail...Lucky Star. I...heed and break to your will."

The captain nodded. "And what will you say, heeding my will?"

The seaman sighed. "There is no Jonah."

With a click, the captain uncocked his firearm, holstering it again.

"Commander. Have this man dragged behind me, to where they hold Lieutenant Tegene. Seaman Radagast will replace him, in irons."

"Aye Sir."

Turning on a heel, Lucky Star strode below deck while calling out.

"There is no Jonah aboard! And no vanished ship disappeared because of one! You heard the prisoner Radagast, and I say he is right to say it! Follow his...lead! You have your captain's word of honor! What haunts us is of this Earth and, like the Earth, will break under our will!"

The last thing he heard, with his commander, the prisoner, and two able seamen to hold him, was the cry of the crew.

"To Lucky Star! Our leader! Our salvation!"

FINAL SHIPS IN THE NEIGHBORHOOD

* * *

The two corrupted seamen, the acolytes of Castor, flanked the door sealing Castor and Lieutenant Tegene away.

Lucky Star knew, so far below, that they had not heard the uproar above.

"Seamen."

"Aye, Captain," said both men in unison.

"I have been told by others that you have discovered a Jonah."

Again both answered together, nodding. "Aye, Captain."

"Lieutenant Castor acted to protect the *Stormchaser*. I will see him. He holds the villain, I have been told."

"Aye, Captain."

"Follow me in. I wish to reward you, alongside him, for your service."

Beaming, the two seamen nodded.

Lucky Star unbarred the door and pushed through.

* * *

"Lieutenant Castor."

The man in uniform, standing with a coiled, dripping cat-o-nine-tails in his right hand, turned away from the naked and bleeding black back of a lithe Tegene. Chains held Tegene tight up against the wall.

Lieutenant Castor nodded. "Captain," answered Castor, nodding with respect.

Lucky Star nodded back. "I have heard you found a Jonah."

"Aye, Captain."

"I believed we had none. I believed the fleet had none. I believed, until now, that I said so within your earshot." He paused. "Should I believe I was wrong?"

Castor flinched. "I acted to protect the *Stormchaser*, and so Her Majesty, Captain. I caught Tegene unaware. I heard chanting in his chambers, so I opened his door. I interrupted a spell."

"What spell, Lieutenant Castor?"

"The spell to call the black devil's rock that rises from the depths of hell and sinks even the greatest ships!"

"Ah."

Lieutenant Castor laughed, feeling momentum. "I got lucky, Captain. Not as lucky as you. But lucky enough. I apologize for acting without orders, but you were in the nest. And you never wish to be disturbed. I knew we could hold him. It was for the greater good!"

Lucky Star paused for a very long moment. He extended a hand. "May I have the whip?"

"Aye, Captain."

Behind Lucky Star, the commander cleared his throat. Lieutenant Castor handed over the multi-barbed, feline whip. Somehow it felt not just feline but feminine. The captain examined the blood on its ropes and hooks, and then studied the blood dripping from Tegene's ripped back to pools on the floor.

Tegene moaned. The air smelled of copper.

"Is this true, Tegene?"

"No, Captain. Lieutenant Castor lies. He remembers his mother, who—"

"Silence, traitor!" Lieutenant Castor cried. "Do not dishonor my mother with your words or honor her black murderer by recalling his memory!"

The captain sighed. Silence fell again, save for Tegene's panting.

"Most often, Lieutenant Castor," began Lucky Star at last, "the harder one works, the more luck one has. It is vile superstition to believe that luck is a gift of executed superstition, or even of God."

"Aye, Captain."

"For luck, one must be one's own god."

The captain, letting the bloody whip fall to the oak floor at his feet, turned and beckoned for Lieutenant Castor's followers to leave.

"Stand aside, Lieutenant Castor."

The two men left, but Lieutenant Castor stood in perfect position between Lucky Star and Tegene. The stance seemed, to the captain, protective.

"Take a step to the side please, Lieutenant Castor."

"Aye, Sir."

Drawing his pistol, Lucky Star fired three times, each time splattering Tegene with Castor's brains.

* * *

"Release Tegene."

Commander Pillion shook as he fetched the key from Castor's corpse, unlocking Lieutenant Tegene. Seaman Radagast moaned, eyes rolling. One of the men who'd come down in support of Radagast eased Lieutenant Tegene to the floor.

"Call the ship's surgeon," the captain said to another supporting seaman. "And Commander Pillion, have the other man help you chain Radagast to the wall. Do not slip and injure yourself in the gore."

The commander nodded and, with the seaman who had not gone to fetch the surgeon yet, chained Radagast to the wall.

Lucky Star knelt by Lieutenant Tegene. "Lieutenant. I'm sorry Castor failed you. Superstition, it seems, creeps even into the officers. Is there anything I can do for you before the surgeon arrives?"

"No, Sir. Thank you. You have done enough...Captain."

"As you wish." Nodding, the captain tried to penetrate the blank look of the man. He failed, and so blamed Castor's devastation.

Devastation makes impenetrable piles of rubble.

Rising, Lucky Star departed.

* * *

At the helm of the *Stormchaser*, Captain Matthew Starbuck held aloft his telescope and scanned the horizon.

The red sun sank low, readying to set.

"Is Lieutenant Tegene comfortable, Commander Pillion?"

"Aye, Captain. He is alone in his quarters, resting."

"The surgeon believes he will make a full recovery?"

"Aye, Sir."

Lucky Star grunted. "Good. The surgeon is an intelligent man."

The sounds of the sea and the wind reigned, both battering the hull.

And then something happened. The ocean seemed to take a mighty earthquake of a breath. Air throbbed, and Lucky Star stiffened.

"What?" The captain raised his telescope again, staring dead ahead.

FINAL SHIPS IN THE NEIGHBORHOOD

Far off in the distance he spied a blue, rippling distortion of waves. Out of it, rose something large, craggy and black, as if from the depths of hell below Triton's distant floor. Spikes and hooks decorated it.

It appeared to come from nowhere and, with an inaudible rumble, somehow felt by all in the bones. It blocked the low red sun, setting it too soon.

Lucky Star's heart clenched in his chest.

"Enemy dead ahead! Move broadside! Ready the cannons!"

He tried to spin the wheel.

Nothing. It would not spin, locked and impotent.

And darkness lay dead ahead. The captain sighed, his mind racing.

"Furl the sails, Commander Pillion. Drift to a halt."

"Sir?"

"Do it. Do it now."

"Aye, Captain."

But frozen by some magic, the sails would not furl.

"Commander, send a man to Tegene. Now!"

"Aye, Captain."

Moments later, the man returned.

"Tegene's door is sealed, Captain! By black magic!"

The captain breathed deep.

The Jonah's door.

Lucky Star stood back from the wheel as if stepping back from the queen herself.

"*Stormchaser* soon sinks, Commander Pillion. Abandon her." He straightened. "But I go down...with her."

He handed the commander the telescope. At the same moment, the sharp snapping of ropes rang out over the deck, and the lifeboats plunged to the sea. Cries echoed from able seamen everywhere.

153

"It's breaking apart!"

"We're sinking!"

And another echo cascaded.

"It's the Jonah!"

Lucky Star closed his eyes, forgetting his hands as they clenched white. But they did not break the African oak, the stuff of imperial *Stormchaser's* wheel.

An Afterword to this story is on page 210.

15

ARK
by
Andrea Luquesi Scott

We are all dead.

The details don't matter.

There is no happy ending.

This is the first thing you should know before deciding whether or not to continue reading. I'm not going to sugar-coat things just so you don't have nightmares tonight. If you want the truth at any cost, then read on.

Time in our 3D reality is but a mere construct. A holographic representation of simultaneous events have been squeezed together into a linear mould. There is no time, not really. Everything is happening all at once in infinite directions within our legitimate multi-dimensional existence. I know that now.

It makes no difference, however, because nothing can change what is meant to be. And nothing can change the calamity that is before us—a calamity upon all of humanity.

***

The gargantuan asteroid was picked up initially as a faint echo by SETI pre-warning scanners twelve years before scientists predicted it would hit. The determined scenario was nothing short of an extinction level event. Nothing would survive. But even if the world's greatest minds got it wrong and the asteroid only came within a thousand-mile vicinity of the Earth, the tsunami generated by the planet and asteroid's gravity waves colliding would prove catastrophic.

For once, world governments set aside petty rivalries and pulled their resources to build the most ambitious feat of aeronautical, engineering genius ever known to humankind. The master plan involved evacuating as much of Earth's inhabitants, fauna, and flora as possible, leave before the asteroid was anywhere near its apogee from Earth, and hopefully return sometime in the future so that Earth may be resettled. In the meantime, generations would survive in between space and a handful of remote planetary outposts near Proxima Centauri within the border of the Milky Way. A pretty grim outlook to be sure, but at least it more or less guaranteed the continuance of the human race.

The *Ark*, one-fifth the size of Earth, was equipped with onboard life-sustaining replicators, plus the revolutionary-yet-controversial tachyon drive, which superseded its ion drive predecessor. Traditional ion thrusters utilized electronic propulsion via the acceleration of ions. They were able to reach speeds of up to 321,000 kilometres per hour and could last for five years.

The multi-trillion credit tachyon drive was largely untested in its superluminal capabilities. No one was sure of what it could do until it was initiated. Powered by antimatter, the amount of energy necessary to run it was equal to 1.5 million Hiroshimas. But real public contention lay in its origins. As opposed to its precursor, details of its development were sketchy. It was as if one moment there was nothing to rival the ion drive, and then the tachyon drive arrived to blow it clear out of the water altogether.

***

I gazed out across the expansive launch site. It was dawn. In less than three hours I would be on a transporter shuttle on its way to dock with the Ark, which was hovering a few thousand kilometres past the moon. The trip would take a matter of hours. The watery mist kicked up by Iguazu made it hard to see, but I could still distinguish the silhouette of trees that made up the sub-tropical forest basin with the sun just glinting off its corona. I loved it there. It felt magical. A tear graced my cheek. I found it hard to believe that something so beautiful could end so completely.

Four hours later, I watched from my tiny shuttle window as Earth grew smaller and smaller. *No more camping under the Grand Canyon stars. No more Blackcomb skinny-dipping escapades at 2000 feet. And definitely no more looking out over the Pacific, wondering how far across the water until land, as I buried my toes in Avoca sand.*

Strapped into my co-pilot's seat on the bridge aboard the Ark, I carried out a few last-minute computer checks. Satisfied that all systems were go, I echoed this to my captain with a thumb's up. I was at the beginning of a 16-hour shift and one of five sets of co-pilots. I won't bore you with the history but I was pretty much a genius. I'd been there, done that. I wish I could say that my latest stint was to be the pinnacle of my career, but I figured that was based on having a welcome crowd to come home to. Soon none of us would have a home.

Launch went off without a hitch. We were essentially flying a hollow planetoid through space. We generated our own gravity, since we were so big. I made a mental note to check on the validity of that fact when I had some down time. For now, I was playing the ultimate optimist and looking forward to exploring new frontiers, to coin a saying from a favourite old broadcast. My family was with me, and we would survive. What more could I possibly ask for under the circumstances?

For Earth to survive.

I kept thinking that maybe the asteroid would pass without much incident. Maybe the white coats miscalculated or something. I hoped against hope that I would somehow figure this out, that it wasn't the end. I wondered if, on finding the solution, I would have the strength to do what it takes— no matter what.

***

I awoke abruptly to the sound of alarms ringing. We had been travelling at warp for over two months. We should have been heading towards Proxima, but as I reported to the bridge and checked my instruments, it was obvious that we were not. *Where are we?* Nothing in my read-outs even resembled the star charts for the part of the quadrant we were supposedly astrogating. I was dumbfounded.

A missive from engineering brought us up to speed. There had been a malfunction with the plasma stream. We were essentially powered by black hole energy. It was harnessed and drip-fed incrementally into the core. There was not a minute space for error, as too little was not enough to generate the correct levels for propulsion, and too much... well, we could only speculate. Suffice it to say that we had not tempted the fates in this regard. But maybe tonight we finally had.

It was beyond me how anything like this could happen. I officially relieved the co-pilot on duty and switched off auto-pilot. As soon as I did this, a multitude of lights lit across my control panel.

It's not possible!

I stood, gaping at my terminal, feeling the blood drain from my face. Around me, crewmates shouted directives to one another, each scrambling for clarity in any form. I slowly lowered myself into my seat and held my head in my hands.

It's just not possible!

The drive was partly experimental. We all knew to expect the unexpected. It was just that so much of the unexpected relied on first initiating the drives and waiting to see what happened over time.

And therein lay the clue. *Time*.

No one could possibly have guessed at the scope of infinite interactions the warp bubble we were travelling in would play with the fabric of time and space. And as I hazarded another look at my screen, I finally understood how possible the impossible really was. I typed out a few coordinates and waited for a response. Rubbing my eyes and pinching the bridge of my nose, I rose and exchanged a few words with the pilot and captain. They shook their heads in disbelief. I was past that point. I requested that we open comms for a full visual on my calculations. A holographic screen appeared before us and soon after, a third-dimensional representation of the star field we were traversing.

The bridge fell silent.

There before us, not a few hundred-million kilometres in the distance stood Earth, resplendent in the sun's warm glow, as familiar as anyone knew it from the dark recesses of deep space. A beeping sound jolted everyone into action, except no

FINAL SHIPS IN THE NEIGHBORHOOD

one really knew what was happening or what to do. I spoke again with the captain and he nodded solemnly.

I told you I was a genius. I just wish that this time I wasn't. Put simply, an unforeseen byproduct of travelling at the speed of light via tachyon technology was *time travel*. Be it through human error or otherwise, the automatic navigation system had caused a glitch of the worst kind. Coupled with its new-found wormhole capabilities, the Ark had changed trajectory to match that of the original oncoming asteroid. Except that there never had been an asteroid.

WE were the asteroid!

***

We were living through a real-life time paradox. Somehow, unexplainable and impossible as it may seem, we had already lived through this on first encountering the asteroid. Back then, it was so far away that we deduced that it must be a stray heavenly body on an extended orbit that had finally been caught in the joint gravitational pull of our neighbouring planets. We had no way of knowing that it was a hollow vessel in the shape of a planet. *Us!*

The asteroid was travelling at exorbitant speeds, and it was always clear that its destination was planet Earth. Now that I knew it was us, it would purely have been a matter of changing course to avoid impact. Except it wasn't that simple. Even if we could alter our present path across the cosmos, we couldn't do it in time. The warp we were travelling in had an initiation and destination point. We couldn't decelerate out of the preset sequence without blowing ourselves up, or worse. The whole point of saving humanity would be lost in one swift action.

I ran another succession of calculations based on our current location, speed, and the location of Earth. The good news is that the scientists had been wrong. There would be no impact. Unfortunately, our pass by Earth would be too close.

Space is, for the most part, made up of vast voids between the planets and stars. But alongside these are particle streams, which also travel through it. We were travelling at the speed of light—actually, faster on last check—and feeding our own energy reserves off the energy the warp bubble generated internally. Countless particles are picked up by the gravitational distortion. When the Ark eventually stopped, these particles would continue to be propelled by their own exaggerated levels of inertia, picked up as they hitched a ride along with us. This would cause them to become volatile, high-energy tachyons capable of irradiating anything in their path. Earth would be pounded by an immeasurable nuclear assault of which it could not defend itself against.

So this is where we were…on a collision path with Earth and its ultimate destruction. I couldn't believe the irony of it. As soon as I thought of it, I had to laugh. But it wasn't a happy laugh. It was an uncertain and stake-through-the-heart kind of moment.

Did I have the strength?

It wasn't my call. I wasn't the captain, after all. I didn't have the lives of billions of humans in my hands. But then, maybe I did. Again I approached the captain and pilot. My morbid suggestion couldn't have been described as anything else. In my head, the logic seemed sound, despite the illogical state of affairs we found ourselves in.

Earth's best chance for survival on discovering impending doom from the incoming asteroid was to evacuate via the Ark. It was then determined that we, ourselves, aboard the Ark were said asteroid and Earth's initial cause for concern. It then stood to reason that if we were to destroy the Ark, the original threat to Earth would cease to exist.

I played out various scenarios over and over, and each time I encountered a different set of *what if* questions. Such was the nature of the paradox. Aboard the Ark, I was branded nothing short of mad. And I suppose I was mad to even consider it. But what other choice did we have?

***

I stared at the stars from the main window on the bridge. We all did. Far in the distance, a tiny blue dot pulsed gently... *Earth*.

***

I gazed out across the expanse of rocky outcrops to the valley below. It was sunset. From my perch atop a dusty red cliff, I realised why we called it the Grand Canyon. Here on Earth, the vista was one of the most inspiring. Magical. I stood and dusted off my jeans. I bent down and looked through the eyepiece of my telescope. Away from bustling city life, the stars were the most brilliant and clearest to view. A tiny glint caught the corner of my eye and I honed the scope's digital sensors towards it.

Supernovae.

A tear graced my cheek. I found it hard to believe that something so beautiful could end so completely.

An Afterword to this story is on page 211.

16

TO ANACREON IN HEAVEN

by
JD Mitchell

Shedron heard the *PINGS!* against the metal hull of his craft, before he even saw the approach trajectories register on the dumb-puter of his even dumber, and more antiquated, space shuttle. Magnetic wave signatures appeared on the sound-speakers, *PING! PING! PING!* Then he saw thick red lines on a blue graph-field of charged photons. It all meant the same thing: death, destruction, his body torn to pieces, or thrown from his craft. Explosive decompression made things messy inside a torn suit.

Shedron had encountered the problems beyond the Moon's orbit, too early in the mission for his liking. The first mission out of Cislunar space would be a thing to remember. Or the last. He was sure about a few things. Before this flight he located the magnetic minefields. Hence, he found a plotted-route between the known minefields, safely into the gravity-well of his first destination, *Pallas* the asteroid.

Yet common knowledge throughout the Imperium spoke of the existence of other powers, shadowy cabals not content to sit and wait for Earth to obey the Great Partition. Efforts to enforce 'no migration' had seeded the space between the Moon's center of gravity and deep space with autonomous projectiles. NEOs were really just refurbished near-Earth asteroids, *jurisprudent killers.*

His pre-flight preparations involved some work to locate these infernal devices. He had finally found one. Or rather, the NEOs had found him.

Shedron turned off the autopilot and gripped the hand controller clumsily in his gloves. Feeling glad he still wore a suit, he rerouted all power. The age of this ship meant nothing could be wasted or chanced. Energy for life support was redundant. He was from the Dakotas. He would survive.

Air pumped into his suit and the internal temperature was readjusted. Console light-bars signaled powered-down systems and non-biological levels inside the ship. Great for that. Now all electrical systems went exclusively to navigation and propulsion.

His first turn of the hand controller sent signals to the yaw-jets. The old space shuttle's superstructure obeyed. Barely, he imagined. It worked and for a second, the black of space and its maw of stars pitched wildly in the flight deck's forward windows. He strained against disorientation and fired a few more blasts of the yaw-jets. Once again, Russo-soviet technology proved the doubters wrong. He chucked inside his helmet to think that he had partly chosen this ship to spite the Revivalists. Then he remembered he had a good chance to die.

The issue that pressed him was logistical. For he could spare none of the main fuel from his larger engines. A true successful mission meant a return to Earth.

Alternatives did exist, however.

He reached up and threw back an overhead switch and its

master. Suddenly the dumb-puters chimed, in-question. Did Shedron mean to vent all the oxygen?

Not all, and not all at once. But he did set the dial to conserve some and bail the rest, but in controlled bursts. Angles and rates of escape. It was all too much to calculate, much less program. So he would go with the easy way. Out in space, ups and downs really meant *all-arounds*. His decision was to point the space shuttle backwards, so the stern-side was the frontside and the direction they went. Shedron only needed to vent oxygen in one direction and punch in each moment to release. Not yet. He had a few hours perhaps until he approached the neo in-chase. Until then, he could catch a quick nap.

With halted breaths, the only thing he minded now was his higher mind beginning to grow dull....

When he awoke, his mind and hands swung into action. The dumb-puter screamed. A chorus of *PINGS!* rang through his helmet. He turned off a switch. Silence. His eyes went to the thick red line that nearly took up the entire field-graph. The ship he piloted, nearly there, and the neo still on-route. He punched each button, oxygen in each pod was vented, and then the ship increased in speed. Numbers flew faster in his head than the dials on the console. When predicted and real-time calculations equaled each other, he grabbed the hand controller for one final adjustment.

With the punch of a button, he fired the rocket anchor into the surface of the killer asteroid and in seconds, the tether unraveled. Seconds more, and the space shuttle began to whip around, while sling-shot energies took over a new path. A sort of new launch.

Exposed to new gees, he farted.

The worse thing he could imagine was not the smell in his

suit. From what he knew, the place would smell worse on the return trip home.

***

In Shedron's sleep, considerations of the long line of intrepid pagani consumed the animal activities of his dreams. This saddened him. In the context of his ancestors, he would be the last.

Here is what he knew: the first Celestial Engineeri went this way. Most of the Consciousable world called Julian Buren the Second, *Junior.* most affectionately.

But he undertook those missions for the glory of self. The expeditions visited the moons of Mars, and then its deserts. Next came the biggest worldlets in between, before the Crown Jewels of Jupiter and the act of history when the Galaxi clones walked on new soil and ice. Finally, the children of the expeditions spun off to the ringed world, to disappear under the clouds of Titan or to drink in its sea of dreams. Lost.

That was glory to dream of, and not a tired, lowercased-earth now depopulated and depleted, but a home for him, Shedron Tau Ceti, the last of a line.

***

"Like those lines."

Nipponese was easier to understand in the first moments he awoke. The voice came faintly to his ears, submerged in the squelch of static from the sea of charged solar particles. But he clearly heard a female speaker. A greeter before his dawn of arrival.

A whiff of the smell of canned skin-in-a-tube made him

gag a little. He drank water from the straw in his helmet, probably his sweat and urine. He was a universe unto himself now.

Confident his mouth and throat could make human sounds after the long meditation on deep space, he addressed the faceless voice, aware that his own voice contained the right amount of neo-cola classicism but at a minimum. They needed to know the authenticity of his origins. However, he and the rest of them belonged to the defeated side, after all.

"On a fast train to the readjustment of Ceres," Shedron said. "Von Strauven Imperium spacecraft, *Ptichka,* sponsored by Octopi Incorporated, but of course."

Even the static died. But Shedron knew they waited and while he waited, his ship and him flew alone toward their destination.

"That's...that's a mouthful. Do...I have the honor of speaking to the T'Tauri?" she asked.

The gulf of space created many impossibilities. That the children of partition would know his name-from-exile seemed improbable at best. As he sped towards Ceres he guessed that her keen eyes and instruments had spied his lonely trip across the void. But more likely his benefactor, Hirohito on his Seraphim Throne had announced prior to some if not all the divided worlds of the arrival of his chief scientist.

So the dark did know.

"I didn't think I'd find you camped out on Vesta. Are you the advance guard of exile?" Shedron said.

Hirohito's claim over his possessions gave him the right that very few could boast. Only the Emperor, the victor of a great murderous frenzy, flew at will toward the populated planets. And even those sojourns were brief and by all accounts nothing special.

FINAL SHIPS IN THE NEIGHBORHOOD

The speaker's words floated on flares of static.

"Seeing you hurtling...like this...reminds me of...that little girls' school...in the Yamato State," she said. "I drew a ship like yours once...and I really liked it."

Shedron took a breath and a sip from the straw. To speak to an old girl who had once put a dagger to his neck. "I can almost guess the rest, sister. Some boy ripped it up."

"I've already sent a neo after you, but before...before you go, I want you to tell me, while we can...talk simultaneously like this, over—radio contact—tell me why you—"

Static turned to silence and through the flight deck windows, he could see with the naked eye the glitter of an inbound object. Stealthed to radar. Defenders of the Yamato-state extraterritorial-alities brooked nothing. Not with space on fire.

"It's your brother, I'm afraid," Shedron said. "He's never given up the old *maki* who bore you both. He carries on her vision. So I'm going to Ceres, where there's something he wants very much."

"I see," she said. "There's a swarm of natural...debris fields wrapped around Ceres—asteroids. It's the readjustment of Ceres that did that. But you probably knew that, you sly prick."

He laughed, for he did know of the asteroids pulling along with Ceres. And she did know him well. This unintended consequence was pretty much planned. What magic disaster-from-the-skies could work on the incorporated lords of the Imperium? If not for a killer swarm of asteroids, would the Futuriens have allowed this mission?

That did not matter now. He had left from Big Hawai'i on an antiquated Russo-soviet space shuttle just in case. For this appointment was much delayed. Almost by thirty years, she had waited to sow Earth with an animal. One thought to be extinct.

"Never thought I'd talk to you again, Sachi."

"When did we...see each other...last time? Oh yes—"

"The last, real race of the Americas, that's right, before the intrusion of the Games Committee. Before El Pepsi!"

"In my summation, it was...the entry of the Prince of Pepsi-country...that made the games more fun," Sachi said.

"I guess it depends which side you were on."

"I'm sorry, Shedron, but either way you look at the end of those days...you were on the losing side...always."

And before Shedron saw the flash of the explosion, the dumb-puters went mad with klaxon screams. Something about a radiation signature from a captured near-Earth asteroid.

While her words hurt worse, he always had the flick of the switch.

***

One last invention of the ancients, used by the Engineeri, allowed Shedron to live—even survive—his fantasy of space travel.

In the end of history that every golden age is mistaken for, boredom reigned, and where pastoral energies ruled the lands, the bucolic looked to the natural darkness above for inspiration. Adventure awoke not in the west, where the first expeditions of Julian rose to the sky on pillars of flames, but in the east, where the children rebuilt in the shadows of Maximillian's atomic stoicism.

A man from the place of a thousand isles pointed to the points of light beyond the Earth. He chose an ambitious course to the purpose of discovery, to give meaning to the places on the maps of earlier robotic probes. The worlds of the Outer Planets would not only have human features, but imaginary of people's cultural inventions could take root in soils of rock and ice and fire.

From the thousand isles on the Earth's equator, Greatest Malay, his people called him *Zhenghemahesanbao* (Zheng-he-mah-es-an-bao). But it was by the successes of his exploits in the 42 Light-year Fleet that he became *Zheng He the Awesome*.

In the reappearance of history, the first days of that cursed year 2882, his disappearance was recorded after a final voyage into the black (it was not called the 42 Light-year Fleet for nothing!). His lieutenants were the last of the Celestial Engineeri, who wrote for him the *Great Catalogue of Worlds,* and then they faded into the gloom. But one invention lived beyond all, even after his disappearance, the *Zheng-He Field*.

It was evil magic to use subatomic particles to redraw reality. But the field could. For when spaceships were flung outward on the wakes of hydrogen blasts, every attempt to reach sublight speeds needed just a little more precaution.

Some still clung to that method of infernal energies. Shedron thought he would be the last; and with the shield, he could play one last card against the hospitable victors and twisted losers of the war to rule Earth. Perhaps with this technology, a gift from his people, the Engineeri, he could finally win.

***

The *Ptichka* moved by the last graces of the neo's explosion, nose down, its cargo bay doors wide open to embrace the destination world. The majesty of Ceres took Shedron's breath away. Not only because he now spied a world he once imagined as a speck in occulated eyes and mathematical resonances on a map, but for the sight of a world already transformed by a closer orbit to the Sun. More than the frozen seas of the planetoid's world were warmed. He shed a tear and continued to hurtle closer, until he could dock with the slingshot superstructure that flung hydrogen bombs from out of the cowl, shielded by a subatomic virtual-maw.

Zero-gee made the flight and below-deck fun. Last time alone before the life form was on board. Right now he just waited for the robotic claw to grab the space shuttle and pull him toward the protrusion of the thrill-back delivery system. Glimmerings of a subatomic post-code lurked on the quadrants of space. A brief haze in time-space.

Shedron stunk in the same long underwear since orbit around...Luna. For that was the name most would have to use in order to distinguish the Earth's original moon from its newer satellite. He persisted in his thoughts on this matter. The work to cycle the airlock and step outside was old news. When he jumped from one superstructure to another, he then began to think about Ceres' new home. Orbital insertion would be the easy part. The tough work was nearly over. Nearly past the point of no return and the drama of a solar system that frowned on migration between worlds, much less than the movement of one world to another.

Handholds down the webs of metal rigging allowed him to crawl down to the surface of Ceres. The white surface of its frozen seas yawned before him. One hand pull after another marked his pace down the scaffolding. For a minute he could feel the barely perceptible gravity of the planetoid. It seemed to pull him close. He must have imagined it, for Ceres had tugged on his imagination long ago.

He let go and floated the rest of the way down to the surface. The first footfall on a new world carried none of the expectations one might have of such a place. It was barely a slag of superheated ice and a once molten core, spun into a sphere of ice. But even the first steps seemed softer, the thin sheet of dust almost ready to sink into a melted mix from the warm rays from the Sun, the seas beneath almost ready to churn again. He knew he imagined this all. Ceres still bore the memory of millions of frozen years. The place would carry that weight along time.

He walked out of the shadow of the thrill-back delivery system, and toward a group of space suited workers, Nippon's men and women. Over intercoms they spoke, surprised to see a visitor. He was anxious to get this over with and with waves, they said goodbye.

An upside down pyramid thingee stuck out of a frozen bluff. He trundled toward it, approached it, and entered a door framed by Christmas lights. He knew that was right. She had changed little in her tastes.

Welcome Shedron, you've been missed, you'll have to forgive my appearance, but I wanted to get the chance to bathe in these waters. Cometta's thoughts commanded from a hidden place within the building's darkness. *Ceres is like a miniature version of home, and the baby likes to swim in the low-gee."*

Cometta did a strange thing with words in his head. He faced the approach of darkness in a pyramidical-shaped cavern. His suit-instruments still registered a vacuum in the blackness. Cautiously, he turned on his helmet's lamp and spied a wall of ice in front of him. A human form swam in frothy currents. Cometta stopped and waved, her long black hair suspended behind her and fully spread out in the form of a black sail.

FINAL SHIPS IN THE NEIGHBORHOOD

You look so uncomfortable, Cometta thought, *like you haven't taken off that miserable suit since the beginning your trip.*

Shedron smiled, fully envious of the meta-female.

"How's your leg, Gran Dame?" Shedron said.

She hovered in the passages of water behind the ice. "I won't be going back to Earth ever again, which sort of pains me, you know, like, it's for real, and I'm never going back."

He laughed. "Why are you speaking like a modern?" He clearly saw her eyes widen behind the panel of ice.

"It's not for me. It's for 'him'. He needs to talk like a Californian, you know, like totally, if that's where he's going to go."

"I thought we decided on Oregon?"

Bubbles escaped her mouth, in mock laughter to the real sound in his head. "Please, Shedron, that'd be too obvious."

***

Out of dock from in-bound Ceres and, the next time Shedron would see the planetoid again, he would be on Earth. Much older, probably no wiser. Anything to stabilize the planet's axial tilt.

The old space shuttle could be thanked. The job was nearly complete. It only needed to retain the oxygen and fire the engines for two more burns. One to leave Ceres, another to enter Earth-orbit.

He heard the creature make noises. It cried. Cometta had entrusted him with the animal, so no escape, and no better time than now to get over his fear.

Downstairs in the passenger deck, he found the creature in a plastic ball. The sounds out of its mouth terrified him. Gurgles in between long shrieks, then some type of mucus

173

from its nose. He feared it would suffocate and die. With care he took the animal out of its zero-gee bubble and floated to the top-deck. Since the thing was hungry, he obliged it with a baby bottle. He finally looked at the gray-eyed monster and it gazed at him. And sighed.

"To Anacreon in Heaven, indeed...you actually don't smell that bad."

Through the cockpit window, Shedron saw a glint of light reflecting off a celestial body. It tumbled. Another near-Earth asteroid in the grip of Ceres. That was Earth's problem now. He already had his own.

An Afterword to this story is on page 212.

17

GRAVITY UP

by
JZ Murdock

My view of the Atlantic Ocean was unimpeded. The sand was cool and inviting in the afternoon shade of the crushed hull of the US Coast Guard Cutter. I sat, leaning back against the cold steel of the boat and feeling safe for the moment. The shade felt good. I took another swallow of the Johnny Walker Blue, tasting the good smoky-apple flavor, and then rested the bottle on my leg. I closed my eyes, placing my head against the thick steel of the cutter.

After a minute, I looked up at the empty blue sky, searching. Assured that it was indeed empty, normally odd for this time of day, I relaxed, closing my eyes once again. It had been the most significant appointment in my life, and it was meant to be happening. I checked my wristwatch.

I'd worked for two years toward a final meeting with the Janzen Corporation. I had done it. The time had finally arrived! I only needed one final meeting, and I'd be in, no doubt about it. One of the Janzen execs told over drinks that I'd get in—was it only a week ago?

I grinned at the irony of it and took another slug off the nearly empty bottle. It all happened while I was in the store, getting this fine bottle of lovely Irish whiskey. It was a very hot Florida day. Not unusual, really. I wasn't so much thirsty as I was, mentally thirsty. I guess you could call it that.

I was just happy to be sitting in the shade. Just happy it was back, the sun, that is. I ran over it all again in my mind. I reached my arm out and patted the steel and paint of the Coast Guard Cutter that only a few hours ago was afloat out there somewhere, I would presume. Now it was a couple of hundred yards inland from the ocean it once patrolled.

It started with a fog a few days ago. I hadn't seen anything. No one had. Just a gross overview of what happened and yet, it was all so terrifying to me now. I realized my rate of breathing had increased, so I slowed it down, trying to relax again. My thoughts pushed the mouth of the bottle in my hand back up to my lips, and I sucked out some more of the wonderfully numbing liquor.

First there was the fog. It was a thick fog of a kind where you couldn't tell for days whether or when it was night or day. Before the power went out, someone said it was worldwide. Before that, I heard on the news that there was something in space approaching us, something big, like half the size of Earth. They thought it was an asteroid at first, but then it had changed course, heading toward us. Was it a spacecraft approaching, they conjectured?

And then the fog hit. No one had time to be scared before the fear hit or before we started to make connections. Then darkness arrived today. Not like the world turned dark, like night simply came on and forgot to leave. It was how it arrived, like the entire Earth was being encompassed in a shell. There was an advancing wall of darkness that you could see through the fog as frustration rapidly withdrew, quickly dissipating fast as the darkness advanced upon us. I could hear it. Just before the darkness set in, came the lightness as if gravity simply ran out. Before the lightness took over, I felt an unfamiliar cold, a bone-numbing cold.

I shivered. Lost in the moment, I looked around and snapped out of it. I could see the sand. After looking up, I saw the ocean. Out on the horizon, there was a big ship. Usually, there would be many ships out there in the traffic lanes. On the way here, I had walked by two guys who had said they heard there were only a few ships left in the world that could still travel. Rumors, most likely. But out there was clear evidence that at least one serviceable ship had survived. But, how?

Those two guys had that same stunned look I know so well. They looked like zombies, going through the motions, trying to find sanity after our world shattered. Either the lightness or the cold had killed just about everything. At this point, there had to be a portion of the entire world's population left. This part of Vero Beach was usually pretty busy. As far as I can see, there was no one, and there had been no one on it for a while. It was just me, those two guys who were saved by a similar fluke to mine, and one other but.... well he's gone now, too.

I hope some women survived. Now, that was a depressing thought. I took another slug off the bottle. Here's what happened. I had just walked into the ABC Fine Wines & Liquors store, entering through the fog when things started to move fast. It was obvious someone had been taking things from the store because sections were empty, but there were still plenty of bottles on the shelves.

Once inside the store, I heard a noise from outside that seemed to emanate from everywhere. I looked out the windows and doors. The fog seemed to be breaking up. So amazed, I stepped outside and looked toward the beach in the east. I could see someone through the fog across the street, but he didn't see me. He too was looking toward the ocean.

Though I couldn't see through the plants and palm trees in the distance, up high I could see a massive wall of darkness approaching from far out in the ocean, and it was coming fast. A little freaked out, I quickly backed into the store and once inside, kept backing in until I was in the middle of the store. It became very quiet, completely silent.

Then, the lightness came. At first, I thought I was feeling faint and was going to pass out until I realized it wasn't just in my head when my feet left the floor. I saw a wall of darkness as it passed by, and I could see the man across the street quite clearly. He floated upward toward the sky, and then vanished as he passed the top of the glass doors and left my vision.

I was about halfway up to the ceiling when it started to get cold, very cold. I could feel my outer layer of skin start to freeze. I heard what I assumed were bottles exploding as they rapidly turned to a solid block of ice. Below me, liquor was freezing solid.

I could hear odd sounds from outside that I could not make any sense of. I realized later it was the sound of things not bolted down, rising up into the sky: street litter, garbage cans, animals, cars, trucks, boats, trailers, food trucks…and people.

Normally there would be hundreds of people on the street but nowadays, there were only a few out and about, anywhere. People were scared and hording. Only idiots like me or those searching for food were out and about. Emergency services had shut down. We were on our own.

Before I touched down, or up really, I stopped there on the ceiling. I guess I was lucky because the ceiling stopped my rise, but it wouldn't stop anyone outside. The realization froze my thoughts. Suddenly the realization of what I saw, what it really meant, hit me. I felt the terror course through my body, but I fought the rising nausea.

As I touched the ceiling, I tried to hug the panels that were usually held in place by gravity. The panels moved easily up past the false ceiling and into the sprinkler pipes among electrical and HVAC elements that normally carried heat or more typically here in Florida, cold air. I took in the once hidden ceiling as I headed into unfamiliar territory.

That was when the darkness overtook me as it passed the building, moving on to where, I don't know. Would it encompass the entire planet? Everything was dark, a darkness you could almost feel. As I clung to the framework of the false ceiling, there was movement below. Something was trying to come in from the dark outside. It didn't seem to like the sea of broken glass very much, or maybe it was the alcohol in the air, or maybe it just didn't like Crème de menthe. Smells from all different kinds of booze blended together and was becoming sickeningly overwhelming.

I let go of the ceiling frame, trying to get higher above but I was pushing through things that had once sat on the store shelves below me. I ended up against the part of the HVAC system that would usually generate a lot of heat, but the power had been out for days, so that proved useless. Still, I found I was in a pocket high up in the ceiling where the heat had risen, and the surrounding structure radiated some degree of protection. I needed to get away from the bottles that had either frozen and shattered their container so that they were now just bottle shaped lumps of ice or were still rapidly freezing up.

I scrambled upside down along the ceiling to a kind of cubbyhole I had seen just before the darkness took over, absorbing all the light. I hoped I might be a little bit more protected from the cold and from the things that tried entering the store. Bizarre clicking sounds echoed all about as in a vast chorus of macabre musicians, marching, sliding, and moving out of step through the streets.

In the far distance, I could hear faint screams of terror or screams of pain, which seemed to go on forever. I began to think it would never end. Though, I suspect it didn't go on as long as I thought. I was starting to stiffen up from the cold. It was getting to me quickly and at that temperature, I couldn't possibly last very long.

Then it suddenly ended as quickly as it had arrived. My weight returned. I dropped heavily into the ceiling panel framework where I got a bit hung up as other things pummeled me on their way to the ground. They passed me by and made a horrendous sound of crashing and shattering glass and a splashing of liquids. Apparently luckily, I thought ingeniously, not all of the bottles had frozen after all. Maybe some were still intact. The smell of alcohol was thick, rife in the air.

I grabbed the ceiling as I fell so that I ended up hanging from the framework. I breathed a few breaths, then located a fairly safe place to land that was, luckily right below me, and let go. I dropped to the floor, slipped, did a little dance in trying not to fall into a vast sea of broken glass, and remained upright. Though I realized that, had I fallen, I supposed the alcohol would have helped in staving off infection.

FINAL SHIPS IN THE NEIGHBORHOOD

I was stunned at the devastation around me. Carefully, I stepped to the front of the store. It was silent except for the sounds of dripping liquids all about and my crunching glass as I strode forward. I finally stepped through the front door in order to take in the neighborhood. The darkness disappeared, and the sun was back out. After the intense cold, the darkness, and days of fog and no sun, its intense heat was blinding and overpowering.

I looked across the street and saw the man I had noticed before, looking at me. He had survived by grabbing the palm tree as he floated up. He was sitting in the top of the tree, probably trying to figure how to get back down. The thought of falling forever upward into the sky was truly fear invoking.

Then, I heard it. I could see that he heard it, too. We both looked around, then at one another. The closest thing I could relate it to were the sounds I had heard a few minutes ago as everything was lifted off the ground and up into the sky. I could see that we both realized the same thing at the same time.

We both looked up. At that moment, I learned what it was like to feel absolute terror. Everywhere I looked, things were scattered throughout the sky that left shadows on the ground in the most eerie way. They were all growing larger. I realized I was in a shadow, too. It chilled me, the sun being blocked, momentarily. The shadow moved off of me and slipped across the street over to the man.

Everything that had fallen up into the sky was now on the way back down, along with some huge structures, the biggest and the heaviest seeming to be arriving first. There was an oil tanker ship in the distance. I saw airplanes, semi-trucks, cars, and smaller objects—debris and pieces of building that weren't locked or nailed down. Then things started crashing all around us.

The man across the street panicked, trying to find a way down. I realized that the shadow that had been on me was still on him. Suddenly, a semi-truck landed right on top of him, crushing the tree to the ground with him beneath it. Terrified, I turned to run back into the building but had the foresight to look up first, which was the only thing that saved me.

I saw what had to be a yacht just as it touched the roof of the store and landed directly in the center of it, blowing the windows out at me. I had just enough time to leap to the side, away from whatever would rocket out the windows and doors. The sound from the explosion was deafening, and the flames shot out past me into the parking lot.

The noise and explosions continued on as things all around were falling, making it sound like it was one long drawn out explosion that wouldn't stop. I was being peppered with debris that shattered upon impact and spread out sideways, in some cases, for great distances. I looked up to see if I was about to be crushed, but the yacht seemed to be my only contender. It took about five or ten minutes for the last item to hit the ground; I'm not sure really, as I lost all sense of time. Then, there were the people. Frozen people, who shattered upon impact; a few simply driven into soft ground like croquet stakes.

Finally, I stood back up, brushing myself off, and listened. There seemed to be silence now, and the sky seemed clear. I could hear random explosions from all around the area. In the distance, there were larger explosions. I had been lucky. Very, very lucky. I looked across the street. There was red on the pavement coming out from under the semi, from the man I had only momentarily exchanged a final look with.

FINAL SHIPS IN THE NEIGHBORHOOD

Going back into the store was a lost cause, so I started walking toward the ocean. I just wanted to see water. As I picked my way through the debris, I found a perfectly sound bottle of Johnny Walker Blue, the expensive stuff. I was dumbfounded and couldn't have been happier.

As I cracked it open, for the first time from my new vantage, I noticed the corpse of the semi-truck driver still in the cab, partially hanging out of the windshield, frozen solid. His eyes were staring right into me, and through me. I took a slug off the bottle while we locked eyes, and then left that store, forever.

So now here I sit in the Florida sun, still enjoying the embracing heat of the sun from the shade and luxuriating in the emptiness of the very blue sky. What else can I do now but sit, relax, and try to ward off the shakes of absolute fear and wonder? *What was all that? Worse, what might be next? Or, is this all there is?*

After a while, I got hungry and tired of just staring out into the ocean, so I walked back toward the A1A highway. I could hear something in the distance. I could tell that it was a very expensive sports car coming my way. It was moving fast as it ripped down the street. He must have been doing about 150MPH if not more.

Then the car veered slightly as it headed directly for one of the immense metal high-power poles that lined the highway like a weird spare linear forest. He disintegrated right into one of the poles. Parts of the car flew beyond the impact point. It was a loud sound of crunching metal and glass and then, nothing. Silence. I bet that wasn't even his car. Maybe I'll venture out to find my own hot little ride and do some cruising of my own.

After all, "In the Land of the Blind, the one-eyed man rules." Right? Now this place might not be Blind Man's Land, but there has to be a lot of newly abandoned, ownerless things just lying around ripe for the pickings. There's more than one way to make it in this world.

An Afterword to this story is on page 213.

18

KRIMA

by Robert Tozer

Jason was late.

He crashed headlong into a deliveryman. Packages and envelopes erupted from the deliveryman's arms and rained onto the hallway's floor. Curse words also erupted from the deliveryman when Jason continued to race on without even glancing back to see if the man was injured.

He arrived at his destination and winced when he barreled into the office door, and it slammed against the wall. The gathered jumped in their seats; many gave Jason a rude look as they settled their nerves.

"Er, sorry about that." Jason quietly apologized. The returning silence unnerved him, and his face turned crimson.

"As I was saying," a very rotund man seated at the head of the table said. The man's face held a look of contempt toward Jason as he continued to speak. "The object continues to hover two miles above the surface of the Earth. All endeavors to communicate with the craft have been unsuccessful, and as you all know, the military's attempts to shoot it down have failed. It's just been sitting motionless up there for seventy-two hours."

"I'd be more than a little pissed off if I were them," Jason said offhandedly to himself." Realizing that he'd spoken out loud, Jason shrunk back in his chair as a new round of smoldering looks shot his way.

Outside, a sulking Jason was leaning against a lamppost. "Well, wouldn't you be if that happened to you? I mean, you travel how many light-years to a planet that has intelligent life, or is supposed to have at any rate, and you get attacked while just sitting there? I wouldn't be surprised if they just annihilated us for being a stupid species. What are your thoughts, Madison?"

"I can see both sides of the coin, Jason. But, kicking you out of the meeting because you couldn't hold your tongue wasn't too professional on Richard's part."

"Yeah, well, Dick has a way of living up to his appellative. What do you think they want, anyway?"

"I don't know," Madison said. "But, they're certainly on another level of being. Like you said, they've traveled however far to get here. They could've contacted us before they entered our atmosphere and invaded our space. You'd think that would be an unwritten law when visiting inhabited planets; eventually someone's going to destroy you for your impertinence."

"Unless they already knew what to expect when they got here," Jason pointed out. "It's hard to keep our planet's military might a secret when we're broadcasting news, movies, documentaries, basically everything about ourselves twenty-four hours a day, seven days a week. Our radio and television signals travel endlessly throughout space in all directions. We've essentially made a beacon for any alien race to follow."

"It's strange that they've kept silent for so long," Madison said with a puzzled frown. "I kind of hope they'll move on without even contacting us. History hasn't exactly been kind to the technologically inferior people that encountered a more advanced civilization; it usually leads to disaster—the American Indians being a prime example. The only reason I can fathom as to why they haven't contacted us yet is because if they *have* intercepted any signals we've been sending out, they're taking time to assess what humans are in person compared to what they've seen on TV. The signals we're sending out act like a time portal. The farthest television signals would be from 1928. For all we know, they may think we're people from a black and white world, singing and dancing at the oddest occasions, or that we all live in tiny apartments and occasionally aim a balled up fist at our spouse while shouting that we'll *send them to the moon.*"

"*Or,*" Jason said with a smirk, "that we spend a good majority of our time getting naked and having *fun* while listening to corny music, if you know what I mean."

"Leave it to you to debase an alien visitation, Jason. You know, you should see someone about that. It isn't healthy to think about sex as often as you do."

Jason looked hurt and sarcastically replied, "Well, at least I think about it in a positive way, unlike some of us."

There was an icy silence before Madison spoke. "You never know when to quit while you're ahead, do you?"

Madison turned and walked away from him. Jason swore at himself under his breath and began to follow her. "Oh, come on, Maddy. You know I have a big mouth when I get upset. It's my coping mechanism for rejection or embarrassment. I really didn't mean anything by—" He stopped a moment to stare at the object hovering in the heavens. "Maddy? Madison!"

Madison turned to face him. "I don't care if it's your coping—"

"Forget that Maddy. Look! The craft is moving!"

Madison followed his pointing finger and looked at the craft. "It's not moving so as much as morphing, Jason. You see. It's getting angular...tapering."

People had begun a panicked exodus indoors once the ship began to change shape. Jason and Madison ran down the block to the Best Buy store on the corner. They raced to the television section and forced their way through the crowd until they had a clear view. Filling the screens was KCTS's anchorman Chet Bromwell. He was pressing a finger onto his earpiece and repeating what he heard. "And I repeat, the mysterious craft is changing shape. Witnesses report there's no sound of moving machinery, just dead silence. All wildlife in the vicinity is evacuating. Thousands of birds are migrating away from the ship. There are reports of rats, raccoons, squirrels, cats, and dogs simply fleeing as fast and as far away as they can."

The camera switched to a live view of the ship and then panned down to a pretty, young reporter who was visibly shaken. She took a deep breath and mustered her courage. "This is Alison Wells reporting. As you can see, the ship is continuing to change shape."

Madison put her hand up as if to plead to a higher authority, and dryly inquired, "They picked *her* to report on the biggest story of all time? That should've been me out there! And all because I wouldn't sleep with Richard!"

"Dick," Jason laughingly corrected. "He likes to be called Dick, remember."

FINAL SHIPS IN THE NEIGHBORHOOD

Madison's reply was lost in some screaming sirens that whizzed by the windows outside. Someone beside Madison shushed her, and Madison grabbed Jason by the sleeve and pulled him away from the crowd.

"What're you doing, Maddy?" Jason protested. "We're missing the event of a lifetime!"

"Oh no, we're not!" Madison growled.

Madison continued to tug Jason along until they got to the escalators where she suddenly let him go. Jason almost fell down the steps, and he reached out to grab onto the railing to steady himself.

"You still have that pile of junk you call a car?" Madison asked.

Jason looked perturbed. "If you mean *Sheila*, then, yes, I still have her. And she's not a pile of junk. Sheila's a classic, 1966 Pontiac GTO."

"She's a classic, pile of junk, Jason."

"She's not a pile of junk!" Jason shouted. He noticed he'd made an echo and lowered his voice. "She's just a fixer upper, is all. Some tender loving care is all she needs."

"Yeah. Whatever. Can *she* drive yet?"

Jason looked even more offended. "Of course! I had her out just last weekend."

"We're going to go to the heart of this story. We're going to get as close as we can to that thing."

"But the army has that area cordoned off for miles around."

"Doesn't matter. I'm going to get this story, even if it kills you, Jason."

It was Jason's turn to be sarcastic, and he overly exaggerated Madison's earlier reply. "Yeah. *Whatever.*"

189

Sheila was being uncooperative, but Jason finally convinced her to turn over. It took them about an hour to travel across town to a fifteen-foot tall fence that skirted a good ten square miles around the hovering ship.

"So why did you bring us here?" Jason asked. "There are infrared cameras, heat and motion sensors, barbed wire, armed guards a couple of blocks away, not to mention that the fence is electric. And not just the shock-the-crap-out-of-you electric either. Remember those kids that got drunk and tried to climb the fence. Three of the four were instantly electrocuted, and the fourth only managed to cling to life for two days in a coma before slipping away. And he never even touched the fence; he only tried to remove his girlfriend from it."

"We're not going over the fence, stupid. We're going under it!"

"Listen, Maddy. If you think I'm going to dig a hole under this thing—"

Madison sucked at her tongue, making a "tsk" sound. "We're not going to be digging under it either. The hole's already there, as in the Duncan Park Reservoir. We used to play there as kids, remember?"

Jason's thoughts churned as he followed Madison through a thick blanket of bushes. Then nodding his head, he smiled at his remembrance. "Oooh yeah. That's where you gave me my first kiss. If I remember correctly, and I know I do, you let me fool around with you on one of those occasions. Maybe I'll get lucky again, hmm?"

"Just forget about that, Jason. We're here for a bigger purpose than your juvenile lusts."

"One of these days, I'm going to think you don't love me anymore, Maddy."

Madison stopped dead in her tracks and turned to face him, an expression of anger emanated from her eyes. "Let's get this straight once and for all. I'm not, nor have I ever been, in love with you. We were friends as kids. We experimented like kids do. And now we're friends in adulthood. Friends! *Nothing else!*"

Jason replied, "Friends with—"

"Don't say it, Jason! Don't even think it. It'll *never* happen!"

Jason's smile disappeared, and his face took on a hurt look. Madison shook her head and resumed her course through the thicket of bushes and trees.

They came across a small clearing. It hadn't been serviced in quite awhile, and bushes and weeds had crept up all around, almost hiding it completely. They reached the edge of a depression where below sat a cement structure built into the ground. Jason helped Madison climb down the steep incline where they stood looking at a large, round tunnel that was gated with steel bars. In the 1950s, it was used as a spring runoff for melting water. Over the years, the climate had changed and the once deep, rapid water had now become a meandering trickle. Madison made her way to the bars, and crept around garbage and a couple of rusted shopping buggies to finally gain access to the corner. There she made Jason move a dilapidated wooden shipping crate that once served as a street person's home.

Holding his nose Jason said, "This isn't how I remember things."

Madison was studying some writing that was scraped into the wall, and didn't pay attention to Jason's comment. She looked over at Jason, who was busy shoveling mysterious black gunk away from an area where one of the bars had been slightly pried out. Her facial expression softened considerably, and she looked back at the writing:

I'LL LOVE YOU FOREVER MADDY - JASON

Madison's name had a heart chiseled around it. In the bottom of the heart was a further etching:

XOX

Underneath the heart, in a small scribble of scratching, was a reply to Jason's statement of love:

I LOVE YOU TOO JASON - MADDY

"Maddy?! You alright?"

Madison quickly turned when she heard her name called. "Hmm?" She deftly moved her body so that it blocked Jason's view of the messages.

"I said, I guess the old saying is true: *You can't go back home again.*" He moved his arm around to indicate how much things had changed since when they'd been there last.

"Yes, of course. You can't go back to the way things were," she said in a voice that was laden with sadness.

"Still think you can get through here, Maddy? You haven't gotten any skinnier over the years, you know."

Madison obscenely told him where he could go.

As they approached the underside of the ship, they noticed that it had stopped morphing. It had changed from a circular craft into a triangle. They watched with amazement as the inky, almost living, blackness of the ship gradually turned into rippling waves of white. That wasn't the strangest thing, though; the craft felt familiar somehow. On some level, deep in their subconscious, they knew this craft had been here before.

"Do you feel it too?" Jason asked.

"Uh-huh," Madison agreed, but not understanding what she was agreeing with.

She unconsciously reached out and took hold of Jason's hand, squeezing it tightly. Jason simply held onto her hand, and for some unknown reason he began to cry quietly. Madison looked at him when she heard him sob, and even surprised herself when she suddenly kissed him on the mouth. Their kiss was deep, long, and full of passion.

Suddenly, a harsh blue light shot down from the ship and enveloped them. They felt themselves being pulled apart, not from each other, but their actual physical bodies were being disseminated. They didn't feel any pain but were shocked to see the other's body dissolving into sparkling dust. For an instant they just ceased to exist, and then they found themselves re-materializing within a room on the ship. They could tell they were inside the ship because of the white liquid-like moving of the room's interior; an interior that seemed to read their thoughts. Alien words began to creep and whisper into their minds. The words touched primal places in their brains. They didn't know it, but sections that were hitherto dormant were suddenly activated and electrical energy surged and sparked across these former unused portions. It was like an awakening from a deep slumber.

"What do you want with us?" Jason asked. He spoke quietly, fearfully.

In his mind, a voice that was his own answered back. It seemed to echo whisperingly soft at first, and then grew in volume until it clearly solidified.

Interests. Amusement. More.

"I don't understand," Madison answered. Jason turned to her with a look of wonder, realizing that she could also *hear* the voice. He couldn't know it, but the voice coming into her mind sounded like her own.

Awareness. Confusion. Love. More.

The pair said in unison, "I don't—" A sudden, sharp pain filled their heads, cutting off the rest of their response. Thoughts were dragged forth unbidden. And just as suddenly, the images and pain ceased.

Why?

"Why what?" The pair continued to answer as one.

Why?

The pair paused while sorting out all the swirling thoughts/images in their heads.

Deny?

"I was afraid," they answered.

Judgment. Failure. Rebirth.

"You can't! What about all the lives? Innocent *or* guilty, everyone will perish!"

Failure. Rebirth.

They felt their minds being freed of the ship, and they ran to each other and embraced. They both felt naked before the other.

"I'm sorry I pushed you away," Madison said, her voice cracking. Jason felt her shoulders shudder as she sobbed.

"Hey. It's okay, Maddy. I understand. I...saw, I guess you could call it, what was in your mind. I never knew you were going through all that crap. If I'd known—"

"No! It's not okay, Jason. I pushed everyone away from me, smothered my feelings. And you...you turned down a scholarship to Yale just so you could be around me? And you did it in the hopes that you and I—that you and I...I see that I screwed up your life as well as my own."

He thought about consoling her, but opted to draw his fingers through her hair and lovingly kiss the side of her head.

"It just seems so unfair," he finally said. "It's going to destroy the Earth because it thinks its *seed* has failed? It hoped we'd become...*what*?"

"I don't know, Jason. It flooded the world and caused an ice age the last time, and before that it detonated something that caused the Earth to remain in darkness for hundreds of years, killing almost everything. I watched as it terraformed this planet the first time it visited here! We've met *Him*, but all I can think about is what I did to you and me. I just wish we had time to put things right. I love you so much, Jason. I—I'm so sorry...for everything."

"Leave it to Maddy," Jason said laughing. "The world has been judged a failure; the sentence: Total destruction. And all she can think about is a lost love."

"It's not lost yet. We still have now." Madison's lips were trembling when she brought them up to his. They shared complete love in that moment.

They began to dematerialize again, and Jason held onto Madison even tighter. This time there was pain involved in their transfer—white hot, blinding pain.

And then they were back.

As the sparkling light dissipated, they heard *its* voice for the final time in their lives.

Gift.

Madison quickly pulled her hand back. She stared at the wall before her. Turning around slowly, she let slip a thin piece of metal out of her hand. The sound of it hitting and bouncing off the ground seemed like an assault on her ears. She rubbed her eyes and stared in disbelief at Jason.

He was young again!

Fourteen-year-old Jason stared in awe at a fifteen-year-old Madison. She had just finished scratching her response to his act of graffiti.

"C—could we have dreamt it all?" Jason sputtered.

"That was no dream if we both remember everything that happened," Madison replied. She beamed a smile from ear to ear. "We've been given a gift, Jason—a chance to do it all over again, but differently this time."

Jason smiled back at her. "We don't have much time, a couple decades at most."

"Then we'd better make the best out of the time we have left."

He gratefully accepted her into his awaiting arms.

An Afterword to this story is on page 214.

1

AFTERWORD

by
Nina Soden
author of

END GAME

Let me first say this, I don't care much for boats. The idea of being stuck on a boat, rocking in the ocean and surrounded by water to the point that land is nowhere in sight, scares me to death and induces nausea. So, when I was told that a ship needed to be involved in the story, I knew my main character felt the same way about boats as I do. Ships, although they still cause us nausea, aren't as bad as boats.

While I typically write from the view of the innocent, the victim, I was excited to step out of my comfort zone with this story. Yes, she appears to be the victim at first, but in the end you find that she is plotting, vindictive, and really the mastermind behind everything that is happening. I had to keep that in mind as I wrote the story, and I believe that if you read it a second time with her real intentions in mind there are clues along the way.

2

AFTERWORD

by
Stephanie Baskerville
author of

THE TSUNAMI EFFECT

The Tsunami Effect is the second short story that I've written with an apocalyptic theme to it. Reading apocalyptic literature allows people the opportunity to explore the consequences of humanity's actions without all the death destruction and mayhem that would actually happen if we faced, say, a nuclear war or, in the case of *The Tsunami Effect*, a bunch of asteroids hitting the earth.

Follow Dr. Jonathan Embers, former astronaut, as he struggles with the knowledge that he is singlehandedly responsible for the destruction of most of the world, with countless millions of people dead (including his wife) and whole countries that have disappeared under water.

Would you be able to bear such a weight on your shoulders?

3

AFTERWORD

by
Timothy Paul
author of

PYRAT RUM

Ambition is an attribute common to people of all classes, races, genders and professions. Shaped by so many variables, ambition may be satisfied through a long, arduous rise through the ranks. Or it may be fulfilled early in life through unexpected opportunity. In this tale of adventure, examples of both distinguish the two principal characters as they become united in purpose. As this tale unfolded on paper, clues to greater mysteries and a larger story unavoidably made their way into the telling. I look forward to a time when I can discover where those threads lead.

4

AFTERWORD

by
Lynette White
author of

A NEW DAY

I did something different with this story. The thing with short stories is that they are not intended to have sequels, usually. In this story, I revisit the survivors of Kinonville and Kingston. When I ended The Incomparable Angie Williams, the survivors were just rescued. It left me thinking, "Then what?" When it came time to write this story, I took the opportunity to answer that.

In this story, the survivors are struggling to start over. When Angie finds herself losing faith, General Condin teaches her a valuable lesson. When I wrote this story, I actually wrote that conversation first and built the story around it. We have all been there when it seems like the entire universe is crashing down on us.

That is when we have two choices: stand up and keep going or curl up and quit. The next time you have to make that choice, I hope you remember the general's advice. May the title alone remind you that the sunrise is coming.

5

AFTERWORD

by
Randy Dutton
author of

FROM BEHIND THE SUN

I love to read and write about science. I'm the son of a rocket engineer and grew up with the space program. So when I conjured up a type of space elevator for another story, I felt I needed more. I wanted to incorporate a version of the space elevator more in line with current designs as a setting. As for the asteroid, I wanted something unique but plausible. The crystalline design that emitted laser-like beams made it more exotic and more dangerous. I thought about making it an alien-designed device but as it ruminated in my mind, diamond lattices in a volcanic pipe came to mind, and what better way to release it from an alien world than to blow up the planet and have solar winds strip away all but the most durable diamonds. The characters were easy since I have a penchant for journalists.

6

AFTERWORD

by
Joyce Shaughnessy
author of

THE APPOINTMENT

I decided to treat *The Appointment* satirically because I enjoy reading the medium. Nelson DeMille is my favorite writer. I only had an idea of the personality I wanted my protagonist to possess, and as the story progressed, I kept asking myself, "What would make this woman even more outlandish than she already is?" I had Olivia running late for an appointment with an editor from a major New York magazine, and while she is driving, she begins to reflect upon how she had reached this point in her career. Olivia never really cares much for the men she easily discards, but she never sees herself as selfish. Instead, she rationalizes everything she does. My goal was to be funny but to make a moral statement regarding selfishness and ambition. Olivia is ruthless on a very grand scale. I hope the reader enjoys reading it as much as I did writing it.

7

AFTERWORD

by
Randall Lemon
author of

ACCEPTABLE LOSSES

Doing one's duty isn't always easy, not even for the strongest of men. How much harder then is it for those of us who are far more ordinary and far less heroic? This is the theme explored by *Acceptable Losses*. The protagonist, Harlow Anders has never been viewed as heroic; maybe not even as competent. Now he finds himself thrust into a situation where it is doubly important that every man do his duty.

The time has passed when he could drift along easily. Now is the time to take desperate measures and the time for men to make hard decisions. Harlow finds that he now has to make a *doozy* of a decision. The lives of his crew and possibly all of remaining humanity hangs in the balance. He makes that decision.

But sometimes having made the decision doesn't end the story. Sometimes living with the results of the decision is even harder than making the decision in the first place. Can an ordinary man live with the consequences of doing his duty?

8

AFTERWORD

by
Gail Harkins
author of

THE SHOOTING STAR

Film footage of meteors streaking through the skies of Russia was fresh in my mind when I wrote *The Shooting Star*. The most vivid images came from the dash cameras that showed fireballs hurtling past a city skyline. That triggered my imagination, making me consider the near misses and the stories of people who were nearly in the disaster zones but, thanks to relatively minor events, were safe.

While writing this, "what if…" drove the plot. Superstitions and the Rule of Three obviously played a role, as did a very sweet but rather weak groom. Not every hero needs to be an alpha male. Men who love their mothers, even if the apron strings are sometimes a bit tight, can make wonderful and considerate husbands (so I'm told).

My goal throughout the story was a certain lightness. I'd call it romantic comedy, but I have no pretension of being a comic. I'll save that for the genuinely funny people of this world.

9

AFTERWORD

by
Andy McKell
author of

DRAGON SHIP

Uncertain about how to approach the theme, I let my mind wander and my fingers type what they wanted. There emerged a mashup of medieval fantasy and star-spanning empires featuring ecological concerns and colonial abuses, with underlying thoughts about legacy and futility. Then came the hard work of fusing these meanderings into an interesting micro-tale. I hope I succeeded. I was pleased to feature three different aspects of the theme word "rock".

The sense of futility came from the strugglings of humans against powers of nature beyond their control, and took a darker turn. Every character runs on the treadmill of his ambitions, unselfish or selfish. However, their fates will be decided elsewhere. The King's death triggers a flurry of plot developments that could launch a novel. Perhaps I will extend the story at some later date. As the characters found out—who knows what the future will bring?

10

AFTERWORD

by
H.M.Schuldt
author of

THE MUD RACE

When I wrote *The Mud Race*, I kept thinking about what it would be like to experience several unpredictable meteor showers that touch down on Earth (meteorites). This curiosity directed me to learn more about what is currently happening in our Solar System when we see an asteroid enter into Earth's atmosphere, seen as a shooting star. The research I found shows that regular meteor showers really do happen each year in real life, during the same months even, and they can last for a whole week.

In my fictional world set in the future, these same regularly scheduled meteor showers have taken a turn for the worse by increasing in size, plunging through the atmosphere, and touching down on Earth, causing enormous damage to ships and buildings. These meteorite strikes and shock waves have wiped out about half of the animals and people all over the whole world. How does life go on? Find out at the Mud Race.

11

AFTERWORD

by
Laura Stafford
author of

THE RISE AND FALL OF KING DABBOLT

In the story *The Rise and Fall of King Dabbolt*, we are able to see the demise of a greedy king through the eyes of an untrusted advisor. The wizard's apprentice is a brave girl for the times she lives in and fulfills her job duties well. But because she is a female, she is not viewed as worthy or knowledgeable. An unfortunate attitude for the king.

12

AFTERWORD

by
Christian Warren Freed
author of

THE LAST DAWN II

This story is the continuation of a small band of survivors struggling to regain their sense of self after near global devastation. It is a lesson in humility and human perseverance. The concept of the story came from an old saying from Benjamin Franklin: "after 3 days, fish and family begin to smell bad." While humorous, it is also true. An old family member who has turned towards the lawless side confronts the hero of the story.

Their confrontation holds the depth of family bonds while struggling to make peace with their new stations in life. What would you do if all you had known fell into ruin in the blink of an eye?

13

AFTERWORD

by
Shae Hamrick
author of

THE MYSTERY OF THE SKINKING SHIPS

After learning of the premise for *Final Ships In the Neighborhood*, formerly called *Mysterious Ships*, I settled on the character of Amber, who had survived a volcanic explosion in the previous book. I placed her in the world that would have resulted from the chaos of several of volcanoes forming at the same time after an asteroid collided with Earth. Using an asteroid required some research as to what types of asteroids there were and which would become meteors. Then there was how much damage they could cause if they crashed into our planet. I decided to put her and her brother, John, on an adventure at sea, searching for a mysterious force that might be sinking ships. It was fun figuring out how it would all come together and I hope you enjoyed the story.

14

AFTERWORD

by
Amos Parker
author of

RESTORATION OF ORDER

This story taps a little into *Moby Dick*, that famous American book few have read because it's such a hard read. Starbuck almost seemed like he'd be the book's main character…except the book didn't want him to be: too noble.

And of course mine is a story about a seagoing ship. And a story about trying to root out the cause of a major problem.

Oh. And it doesn't turn out so well.

The Jonah, on the other hand, is something I got from the movie *Master and Commander: The Far Side of the World*, with Russell Crowe. Is that movie really over a decade old?

15

AFTERWORD

by
Andrea Luquesi Scott
author of

ARK

RSS and I would often stay up until the wee hours deliberating over quantum physics and the unknown, though neither of us were excessively scientifically-minded. That was the inspiration for 'Ark', I suppose, as well as my fascination with humanity's primordial origins, multi-dimensionality and ancient astronaut mythology.

16

AFTERWORD

by
JD Mitchell
author of
TO ANACREON IN HEAVEN

Perhaps the singular event that began *Land of the Ancestors*: the planetoid Ceres becoming the second moon of the Earth.

In the original poem "Epoch," a space shuttle of the U.S.S.R. visits Ceres during its re-adjustment to the Earth. The original motive for making Ceres a second moon laid with three gifts the Emperor Hirohito gives to the Lady Kir-sten'ya, in order to convince her to become his wife.

I am aware that the original Soviet shuttle, the *Buran*, was destroyed in a hanger disaster. However, this story involves making a planetoid the Earth's second moon.

17

AFTERWORD

by
JZ Murdock
author of
GRAVITY UP

GRAVITY UP, is a new story just for this book from the universe detailed in my book, *Death of Heaven*. It is a story from an outsider's point of view, someone with no idea of the worldwide devastation and horror being visited upon the planet and, all around him. It is inexplicable, terrifying, with simply no quick and easy answer as to what is happening to him. Although for us, the answer lies in the book the story is drawn from.

Many stories I write are linked together; from short stories to books to screenplays. In fact, the sequel to *Death of Heaven* will dovetail with the sequel to one of my screenplays, currently a semi-finalist in the competition over at Circus Road Films.

18

AFTERWORD

by
Robert Tozer
author of

KRIMA

What would you do if judgment day really arrived? What if you had the chance to have a "do over" in your life; to be able to change the outcome of your most regrettable decisions? They say that people rarely deviate from who they essentially are. Would you be able to change your life's outcome if you suddenly had an epiphany? *Scrooge* from Charles Dickens' *A Christmas Carol* did. Or would the stubbornness we humans are known for bog you down for a second time and cause you to slip back into a more comfortable and familiar role? On occasion, I've asked myself these very questions. And I decided that if I can't have a do over myself, maybe I can create a set of people who can explore that possibility for me, although, their answers to those burning questions are still not yet fully realized.

Giant Tales 3-Minute Stories:
Giant Tales Beyond the Mystic Doors (Book 1)
Giant Tales From the Misty Swamp (Book 2)
Giant Tales: World of Pirates (Book 3)
Giant Tales: Dangerous Days (Book 4)
Giant Tales: Wrapped In Fur (Book 5)

Giant Tales Apocalypse 10-Minute Stories:
Lava Storm In the Neighborhood (Book 1)
Final Ships In the Neighborhood (Book 2)
Darkness In the Neighborhood (Book 3)

CRYSTAL SWORD CHRONICLES:
GRYFFON MASTER: Curse of the Lich King (Book 1)

FINAL SHIPS IN THE NEIGHBORHOOD

FINAL SHIPS IN THE NEIGHBORHOOD

Made in the USA
Charleston, SC
31 December 2014